I0595561

Hobart Chatfield-Taylor

The land of the castanet

Spanish sketches

Hobart Chatfield-Taylor

The land of the castanet
Spanish sketches

ISBN/EAN: 9783744722865

Printed in Europe, USA, Canada, Australia, Japan

Cover: Foto ©Andreas Hilbeck / pixelio.de

More available books at **www.hansebooks.com**

The
Land of the Castanet

Spanish Sketches

BY

H. C. Chatfield - Taylor

ILLUSTRATED

CHICAGO
HERBERT S. STONE & CO.
1896

Contents

Note

Several of these papers have already appeared in "The Cosmopolitan;" the others have been written simply as sketches of Spanish scenes and character. Being originally intended for a magazine they do not possess the continuity demanded of the chapters of a book. The apology for their publication in the present form is the hope that their perusal may awaken in the reader an interest in a country somewhat removed from the beaten track of travel, whose history is closely allied with our own, but whose people we little understand. There has been no attempt to make the volume exhaustive; it is merely a collection of sketches, and as such it should be considered.

Chicago, September, 1896.

The Land of the Castanet

The Spaniard

IN the evolution of that proud, sensitive, indolent, sometimes cruel, but more often chivalrous race whom we call the Spaniards, the elements of history have been so clearly defined, so varied in their effect, that each era has left its indelible imprint upon the national character.

One often wonders why Spain, the former mistress of the world, a land of such delightful climate and such fertile soil, surrounded by the sea and an almost impassable rampart of mountains, and seemingly possessed of every blessing which nature can bestow, should, after eighteen centuries of glorious history, have fallen to the second rank among the powers of the world, and be the last among the nations of Europe to respond to the influences of the nineteenth century.

The answer is to be read in the pages of her history. There is a limit to the endurance of a nation, and Spain has suffered more than any other land. For that reason she presents the spectacle of a proud-spirited warrior who has struggled bravely against overwhelming odds and has fallen from sheer exhaustion. Other nations have fought and bled and have won their freedom. The Spaniards have fought and bled as freely as the proudest of them, but their efforts have been frustrated. They have never, until within a decade or so, known the blessings of freedom, and since they have been a united nation have not even been ruled by a despot of a Spanish house. They have had despots without number, and they might have endured them had they been of Spanish blood. It is a common saying in Spain that the first Spanish king was the late Alfonzo XII. At least, he was the first Spanish king whose sympathies were Spanish, and whose reign strengthened Spain. Philip II. was morbidly Spanish in his feelings, but his rule hastened the ruin of his country, a ruin from which it has never recovered.

In talking with Spaniards not of the ruling classes, one hears continually that the people are good but that the government is bad. It is always the same story: the woes of the land are laid to the government; and certainly if the successive governments of Spain from the time of Ferdinand and Isabella to the present day could be tried before an impartial jury, no verdict too severe could be rendered.

The people of Spain are good; none but a good people could have been loyal to such rulers, but mere loyalty, pride, or even daring, does not make a people great. There must be energy and activity; there must be commercial enterprise, and these the Spaniards do not possess. Again it is the fault of the rulers. A middle class is the backbone and sinew of a successful nation, and Spain, except in Catalonia, does not possess a middle class. If the Spanish rulers wish to know the effect of a middle class upon a nation, they need look no further than Catalonia; the object lesson is complete. Barcelona, the Chicago of Spain, is as active, bustling, and energetic as its American prototype, and does nearly one-third of the entire importing and exporting business of the Peninsula. But the Catalans are mere shop-keepers, and the Spaniard, if he is not a peasant, must be a gentleman. The middle class has been killed and stultified by legislation and sentiment.

Before condemning or condoning the Spaniard of to-day, it is worth while to review his history and study the effect of each successive era on his character.

The earliest Spaniards of whom we possess any knowledge were the Celts

and Iberians, known collectively as the
Celtiberians. Their history, or its frag-
ments, as told by their enemies, is the
history of the true Spaniards,—a history
of valor and generosity, of restless vigor
and almost heroic endurance. These
have been the qualities of Spaniards in
all ages. In the course of time the trad-
ing Phœnician established himself along
the whole south coast of the Peninsula,
and after the Phœnicians came the
Greeks. But the Greeks and Phœnicians
were merchants rather than soldiers.
For years they made no attempt to ex-
tend their possessions beyond the coast.
About four hundred and eighty years
before Christ, some eager spirits met at
Gadeira and undertook an expedition
into southern Celtiberia. The bold
tribesmen there not only repulsed the
invaders, but they invaded in return.
Gadeira was threatened with assault,
and the frightened Phœnicians applied for
assistance to the Carthaginians.

At that moment the real history of

Spain began,—a history repeated with recurring fatality during the ages. The Carthaginians, like all subsequent foreigners called to aid tottering power in the Peninsula, possessed themselves of Spain. For two hundred and fifty years they ruled the coast; then Hamilcar Barca and his greater son Hannibal overran the Peninsula. Saguntum alone held out. The marvelous resistance of this city marked the first of the glorious Spanish sieges, lasting to the heroic defense of Saragossa against the arms of Napoleon. In those wars against the Carthaginians, the Romans became the allies of the Spaniards, and again the ally became the conqueror. But the conquerors discovered the heroic spirit of the nation they had betrayed in the person of Viriathus, a Lusitanian shepherd, who seven times in the open field routed the Roman legions, and again in the defense of Numantia against the overpowering armies of the republic. This was carried to such an extremity that the few survivors—men, women and children—resolved to die by their own hand rather than that a single Numantian should grace a Roman triumph.

It only remained for Cæsar to complete the work of conquest, and Spain became, in Hispania Romana, a Roman province. The effect on the Spaniard of this foreign rule was so complete that it survives to-day in his language, his laws and many of his customs. The province became completely Roman, giving emperors and poets to the empire, and so thoroughly united to its mistress that it is to-day, more completely than France, a Latin country.

In the disintegration of the Roman Empire Spain fell to the lot of the Visigoths; but the final death struggle was delayed for a time by a typical Spaniard, the devout, passionate, noble-minded emperor, Theodosius, the first inquisitor, the precursor at once of Isabella the Catholic and of Philip II. Theodosius died in 395 A. D., and in five years Alaric was in Italy. While the sturdy Goth conquered Italy, the Vandals and their savage companions devastated Spain. The barbarian host marched unchecked across the Peninsula. What had the Romanizing of the Peninsula accomplished? Where were the Celtiberians and the Lusitanians who for nearly two centuries had resisted the forces of republican Rome? The conquest was more complete, more easily accomplished than that of the Moors three centuries later. The reason for the two conquests is to be found in the system of domestic slavery of the Romans and the Visigoths. A change of masters was a matter of indifference to the downtrodden people; those who were not slaves or paupers were decayed into moral pauperism by luxury.

The history of the Visigothic kingdom embraces three hundred years of debauchery, intrigue and murder. Roman Spain wrought a marvelous change in her masters. They adopted the veneer of civilization in its vices and luxury, and ceased to be warriors. But in those Visigothic days one great question was fought out and settled, seemingly forever —the question between Church and State. Spain was now a hierarchy, in which ecclesiastical influence became all powerful. One great man struggled against this usurpation; but Wamba, the best among the miserable line of Gothic kings, fell a prey to ecclesiastical treachery, and Spain passed under the control of ecclesiasticism, a control cemented by seven centuries of Moorish warfare.

Although scarcely a trace of Visigoths remains in Spain beyond a few ruins and some of their multitudinous laws engrafted into the "Siete Partidas" of Alfonso the Wise, their policy carried on through generations has in more ways than one been the ruin of Spain. Besides developing ecclesiastical power in the affairs of state, they inaugurated the persecution of the Jews, and the Visigothic Metropolitans became the forerunners of Torquemada and his inquisitorial host.

But enough of Gothic rule. It was a decayed exotic which withered before the Arab blast. The enervated Goth fell a prey to his own treachery, and the Arab overran his land. The few remnants gathered in the far Asturias, and raising Pelayo, a relative of the conquered Roderic, upon their shields, proclaimed the first king of a line destined to reconquer, step by step, the fair land of Spain. When Pelayo and his little band of refugees drove back the Moors by hurling stones from their rock-cut cave at Covadonga, upon the struggling hosts below, they inaugurated those seven centuries of incessant warfare which were to be at once the making and the marring of the Spanish nation.

Of the Moors in Spain little need be said. Theirs is a history apart, romantic, fascinating, and seemingly incredible; marvelous in its development, miserable in its decay. They vanished as they came, leaving scarcely a trace beyond the graceful arches and shady courts of their palaces and mosques. But the effect of Moorish wars upon the Spanish character is seemingly indelible. They were seven centuries of crusades; seven centuries of warfare for the Catholic faith. The crusader is a fanatic, and a nation of crusaders developed by hundreds of years of religious wars, must, perforce, become a nation of fanatics. The cross was the national standard; the Church became truly a church militant, for bishops rode at the head of armies, and religion was the dominant sentiment of the nation—hatred of infidels and heretics its dominant passion.

In the mountain fastnesses of the Asturias the banner of the cross was unfurled, and step by step it advanced, sometimes wavering but always facing the foe, until it floated triumphant from the walls of Granada. Except when Charles Martel repulsed the Moor at Tours, the rest of Europe was never threatened by the Crescent. Fanatics and adventurers went forth from England, France and Germany to fight and squabble in the Holy Land, but that was not religious warfare as the Spaniards knew it. In fighting for his faith, he was fighting for his home; to him religion meant existence. Is it any wonder that he became a fanatic, and his land the stronghold of the Church? There could be but one religion for such a people. It was his faith, for which the Spaniard fought, and in consequence the ecclesiastic obtained a power which he has never attained elsewhere—even in Italy itself. The fall of Granada took place but four hundred years ago. Is it any wonder that the religious impetus of those seven centuries should have lasted even to our day? The religious fervor which was excited to inspire the armies has endured, and with it the abhorrence for all that is Mohammedan. It is declared that because bathing was a religious ceremony of the Moor, it,

TOMB OF FERDINAND AND ISABELLA

perforce, became an unholy act for the Spaniard.

With the fall of Granada Spain became a nation. For the first time the many petty kingdoms which had arisen from the remnants of Gothic rule were united in the persons of Ferdinand of Aragon and Isabella of Castile. Only Portugal held aloof, and there was every promise that she too might be brought within the national fold. But the Catholic kings, the creators of United Spain, sowed the seeds of her ruin. Isabella, the sterling womanly queen, whose love for her people and zeal for her Church carried her to the point of fanaticism, and Ferdinand, the crafty, grasping politician, combined those qualities which, intensified in the persons of Charles I. and his son Philip, were to complete the ruin of Spain.

The moment the Spanish Empire was fully created, it began to disintegrate. A century of victories followed, but they were ruinous to Spain. Isabella the zealous, Ferdinand the crafty, each played a characteristic part in the ruin of their country, a ruin they could not foresee, but one which was sure to follow the mistaken policy they inaugurated. The same hand which sent Columbus forth to add a new world to Castile signed the edict for the expulsion of the Jews, and sent two hundred thousand Spaniards, men, women and children, rich and poor, able and infirm, forth from their homes to suffer and die in exile.

Sisenand, the Goth, had nine hundred years before promulgated a similar decree, but he had been too tender-hearted to enforce it. Seven centuries of religious warfare had hardened the heart of even the best of Spanish rulers. The persecution of the Moors, and their final expulsion by one of the weak-minded Philips, was merely a corollary to this act, and finally, beyond these cruelties, came the dreadful engine of the Inquisition. Torquemada, the queen's confessor, whose name is synonymous with cruelty and persecution, was placed in charge, with orders to stamp out heresy, of whatever trifling shade of opinion, and over ten thousand persons were burned alive during the eighteen years of his supremacy. The Inquisition of Torquemada's day was merely directed against the Jews. Yet the sufferings of the Jew and the Moor were but a part of the injury which Isabella's zeal brought to her land. The Jews and the Moors were traders and artisans—in a word, they were the middle class. The Spaniard, on the contrary, was always either a warrior, a priest, or a peasant. The land when bereft of the Jew and the Moor lost that commercial element which is the leaven of every prosperous country. A nation all warriors, priests and peasants can never thrive. One useful class, however, remained—the thinkers.

But Spain was still to suffer a severer blow. Presently the fires of the Inquisition were lighted for the thinkers.

Free thought was refused a place in
Spanish counsels, and with it went the
philosopher, the scientist, and the in-
ventor. Then the soldier, the priest,
and the peasant alone remained. There
were painters and writers, to be sure,
but they painted and wrote to please the
court; they dared not think. That they
were great in spite of the Inquisition
and its horrors was a tribute to their
capability.

All this was the miserable outcome of
Isabella's zeal for her faith. Philip II.
but continued to the bitter end the policy she had inaugurated. But Isabella
was not alone in sowing the seeds of her
country's downfall. Ferdinand, crafty
and grasping, saw in the broad field of
European politics a goal for his ambition. He schemed, and while he plotted
his soldiers fought, until Italy and Sicily
were under his sway. The Austrian
marriage of his daughter brought the
half of Europe under the scepter of his
grandson, Charles I.

The Spaniard

While Isabella with her Ximenes and her Torquemada were cementing the already overweening ecclesiastical power, the Spanish soldiers of Gonzalo de Córdova—"The Great Captain"—trained in Moorish warfare, were revolutionizing tactics on the plains of Italy, and making the Spanish infantry the terror of Europe. A new world, too, was being added to the Spanish crown, in order that its gold might defray the expense of conquest.

The warlike spirit and the fanaticism engendered by the Moorish wars sought new outlets on the battle-fields of Europe and in the Auto de Fé. It was an age of martial glory for the Spaniard, but won at what a price! Conquest for the love of conquest; persecution in the name of religion. The warrior and the cleric were all dominant: the peasant paid the price. Charles I. and Philip II. were but a repetition of Ferdinand and Isabella, save that the one was a greater soldier and the other a more relentless bigot. The one was a foreigner who saw in Spain merely a means to satisfy his ambition; the other a Spaniard who saw in his foreign subjects a means to satisfy his fanaticism. Both continued the ruin of Spain which the Catholic kings had commenced.

When their reigns were over, Spain was exhausted; the soldier and ecclesiastic had held full sway, but there were no more soldiers to fight, and no heretics were left to burn; there was no commercial and artisan class to recoup the resources of the realm. Those whom persecution had spared, financial laws had ruined, so there was nothing for the soldier and religious to do but squabble, and plot, and quarrel. Nothing for the peasant but to toil and suffer. The country was in the unhealthy ferment of stagnation. A good king might have saved the land even then; but instead there came a sequence of three imbeciles from the House of Austria, and a line of foreign Bourbons thrust on Spain through the war of the Spanish succession. One court favorite after another ruled the unhappy land. One province after another fell away, until only the mother-country, Cuba, and a few scattered islands remained.

The Spaniard bore misrule more patiently than his treatment warranted. What good government might have done for Spain was exemplified by the wise internal policy of Charles III. Had his successors been of his own stamp, instead of that of the miserable Charles IV., and the yet more unfortunate Ferdinand VII., Spain might still stand among the great powers of the world. But in those days of her deepest adversity, when her monarch and his son were quarreling, and after seven kings in succession had wasted what few resources the aggressive policy of Charles I. and Philip II. had left untouched, unhappy Spain fought for her worthless royal house against the power of Napoleon as no country in Europe fought.

The French could not conquer the Spaniard, and in the siege of Saragossa the heroism of Saguntum and Numantia was reënacted. It is difficult, however, to judge correctly the history of the Peninsula war. The English authorities scarcely consider the Spaniard, the Spanish writers begrudgingly acknowledge the help rendered by the Briton in driving the French from their land. But of Saragossa there can be but one opinion: there were no British there, and the annals of that siege are among the most heroic in history.

The reward of the Spaniard for his noble resistance was a king, if possible more pernicious than any who had gone before. In the person of Ferdinand VII. were united the worst qualities a monarch could possess, and those he did not have he found in his queen. The latter was the disturbing spirit of the reign of the young Queen Isabella II. She plotted and intrigued, and by her example and teaching made possible the unhappy

GATE AT SARAGOSSA, WITH MARKS OF FRENCH CANNON

ending of that queen's reign. Isabella was not at heart as bad as she has been painted, but she was capricious and passionate, and between Espartero, O'Donnell, Serrano, and the Carlist pretenders, the wretched country was dragged on a steadily downward career. Yet Isabella conferred one blessing upon her country: she founded the Guardia Civil, a gendarmerie modeled after the Holy Brotherhood of her great namesake, an exemplary police, who have made traveling in Spain as safe as in any country of Europe.

The revolution which drove Isabella from her throne, the provisional government of General Prim, the short-lived monarchy of Amadeus, the equally short-lived republic of Castelar, were but the desperation of a people who could endure no more. Ground down by oppression, they struggled to free themselves from their miserable rulers, but the governments thus created so passionately were too quickly formed, though out of them grew a monarchy more liberal, more tolerant than any which had gone before. Alfonso XII. was not an exemplary king, but he was good as kings go in Spain. He was Spanish in his sympathies, and he accomplished as much as could be expected of a monarch whose throne was so unstable. In his wife, Queen Maria Christina, the present regent, Spain has the first requisite of a happy land, a ruler whom the people not only respect but truly love.

Twenty years of peace have been of inestimable benefit to the people of the Peninsula; but the country was in too exhausted a condition immediately to resume its place among the nations of the world. And now comes this wretched Cuban war to arrest again the hand of progress. The Spaniard had not learned in the school of adversity the lesson which should have stood him in stead at this crisis. Had he seen in his own struggles against the Roman and the

Moor, in the revolt of the Netherlands, in his own fight against Napoleon, and in the fight for freedom of his American colonies, the futility of forcing a foreign rule upon a people determined to achieve their independence, this war might have been prevented.

He undoubtedly realizes his error now, but his pride is at stake. Cuba is all that remains to Spain of an empire upon which it was once the boast that the sun never set. Spanish statesmen declared that Cuba must be conquered, no matter what the sacrifices may be. It will be time to talk of needed reform after the greater Antille has been brought back into the national fold. There is a ring of fatalism in this sentiment; it is the cry of a proud but desperate warrior.

The modern Spaniard is the logical outcome of his history. He is proud, sentimental, fanatical even, but not pro-gressive as we understand progression. His courtliness is admirable, but exces-sive. He dwells too much upon the glories of Pavia and San Quintin, without realizing that those very victories hastened the downfall of Spanish power. He dreams of the splendid empire which Columbus and his successors gave to Castile and Leon; but he forgets that there was but one Las Casas, and too many of the stamp of Cortez Pizarro, and Ovando; he forgets that there was but one Talavera, Bishop of Granada, and too many uncompromising prelates like Ximenes and Torquemada. The Spaniard's character has been formed by seven centuries of crusading and a century of conquest. The exigencies of history have made him a warrior, but the incapacity of fourteen bad kings has lost him the power to conquer.

Yet in spite of the influence of past traditions and present sentiment the Spaniard is awakening. Twenty years have wrought marvelous changes in the Peninsula, and though the spirit of the past still hovers over the land,—the spirit which exiled the Jew and the

Moor,—there are many signs which inspire the lover of Spain with the hope that under a more democratic rule she may find the dawn of a new civilization, where victories will be acquired in the realms of art, science, and philosophy, instead of in the clash of arms.

The Capital of Spain

SPAIN'S capital might be roughly
described as a composite photo-
graph of Paris and Washington with two
distinctive features of its own—the Court
and the Puerta del Sol. There is nothing Spanish about Madrid except a few
Spaniards lounging in the sun with
shoulders enveloped in the national capa,
or long, graceful cloak, once so universal but now fast disappearing, or the
devout maidens and demure dueñas
dressed in sombre black, their glossy
hair wrapped in the graceful folds of
lace mantillas, picking their way through
the crowded streets at the hour of morning mass. Except for these and an
occasional Spanish cart with its string
of awkward mules, there is little to
remind one of romantic Spain. There

are, to be sure, the beggars, but the beggars are not picturesque like those of Andalusia; they are merely repulsive and clamorous. The houses, the streets, the life of Madrid, are essentially Parisian on a somewhat reduced scale, while the general aspect of the city is that of Washington.

Like Washington, too, it is a capital of deliberate creation, not of circumstance, and it is merely a capital. Although in the number of its inhabitants Madrid is the largest city of Spain, it is in no sense the commercial metropolis. Indeed, without the Court, the host of governmental officials, and idle people with money to spend whom the Court attracts, it could not exist a day. It is essentially a city of government and pleasure, and the business is mostly confined to purveying to the wants of the functionary and the frivolous.

As a capital, the city owes its existence to the vagaries of two men. Charles V. found that the dry climate agreed with

his gout, and his son, Philip II., could
discover no more dreary spot for the
building of his monastic palace, the
Escorial, than the point where the barren wind-swept plain of Madrid verges
into the bleak, rugged mountains of the
Guadarrama. So the cities of Toledo,
Seville, and Valladolid, naturally fitted
to be capitals of Spain, were deserted,
and the new city sprang into being.

To-day this brightest and gayest of
Spanish towns rises crisp and new in the
centre of a plain almost as barren as the
great American desert. The sun scorches
in summer, the wind chills in winter, yet
for three centuries, in obedience to the
whims of two capricious kings, this city
has grown and thriven in the desolate
centre of a fertile land.

As has been said, the distinctive
features of Madrid are the Court and
the Puerta del Sol. The Court is individual, because it represents the last of
Bourbon power and is swayed by all the
Bourbon etiquette of Louis XIV. The

The Capital of Spain

Puerta del Sol is the centre of Madrid,
—an oval plaza whence the principal
streets radiate in all directions,—a sort
of Place de l'Opera without the opera,
but with more life and movement, for
nowhere do idlers congregate as they
do in the Puerta del Sol.   The name
signifies "Gate of the Sun."   There is
no gate, but there is plenty of sun, and
that is the secret of its popularity as a
lounging place.   The Spaniard of the
middle and the lower classes is never so
happy as when "tomando el sol," taking
a sun bath.   It is indeed a necessity to
his well-being in winter, for his house
is so damp and frigid, with no appliance
for heating except the miserable charcoal
brazier, that the only place he can warm
himself is in the sun.   In fact, the sun is
called the poor man's brazier.

Judging by the crowds which swarm
the Puerta del Sol and the adjoining
streets, the population of Madrid seems
composed principally of idlers.   This in
the American sense is partly true.   The

people do not work as we do. The
shops are opened at nine or even ten
o'clock. The government offices keep
short hours, and the people when not at
work are always in the streets, standing
in groups about the Puerta del Sol or
sauntering leisurely through the Alcalá
and the Carrera San Geronimo—the
principal shopping streets.

In the Anglo-Saxon sense of the word,
the Spaniard never walks (except in
Barcelona where everyone is busy), he
merely loiters, and it is amazing to see
how much satisfaction he seems to find
in this innocent amusement.

There are Anglomaniacs in the smart
society of Madrid, as there are wherever
smart society exists, and they wear London clothes, and walk, and play polo
because Englishmen do, but they are no
more real Spaniards than their prototypes of New York are real Americans.
The daily life of the "Madrileño" does
not begin until noon, and from then until
the early morning hours, unless he is one

STREET OF ALCALÁ, MADRID

of the unfortunates whom necessity
drives to work, he is ever in the streets,
the café, or the theatre. Life is made
cheap enough for him, too, as for the
price of a cup of coffee he can spend half
the day in a café, and the theatres —
except the opera—are so moderate in
their charges that one wonders how they
exist.

The theatres of Madrid are unique in
their way. You do not buy your ticket
for an entire play or an evening but for
one act (or function), or as many acts or
functions as you desire to see. Thus,
to go at the beginning and sit to the
bitter end, at half past one in the morning, requires a handful of tickets, from
which one is collected at the beginning
of each act.

The most popular playhouses are those
where they give Zarzuelas, the national
opera bouffe. These pieces are in one
act or in two short acts with an entr'acte,
in which latter case an intermezzo is
played and the audience retain their

seats. In subjects they vary from the stately court of Philip II. to popular sketches of the Edward Harrigan variety. The music is usually attractive, the book often dull, with too little of the comedy element. The actors are not up to French or English standards, and the actresses are sadly deficient in the matter of make-up, a commendable habit enough for the streets, but not for the boards, where they all look like corpses. At a Zarzuela theatre four distinct pieces are usually given in the same evening—the house being the most crowded during the last. No country is richer in dramatic works than Spain. It has a national drama which is truly great, but as with us in America, the drama is at a rather low ebb owing to the frivolous taste of the public. The Teatro Español is the home of the ligitimate drama and is modeled to some extent after the Théâtre Français, and there one evening a week is devoted to the old dramatists; but the company is only passable, and little attention is given to the mise-en-scène. The theatre itself is charming, and on Monday, the fashionable night, society is always present in force.

One of the many charms of Madrid is its compactness. You can drive from one end to the other in half an hour; the streets in the main are broad, except in the old parts where there is still a dash of local color in the shape of tortuous lanes and hanging balconies; but the greater part of the town is new and French, with straight boulevards well-built houses, modern and monotonous.

The government buildings are situated here and there as they are in Washington—huge modern piles of brick and stone with pseudo-classical outlines, commonplace most of them, in contrast with the noble monuments of the older Spanish cities. The Senate Chamber is an old monastery rebuilt and modernized since 1835, but so completely transformed that one looks in vain for signs of the former cloister. The hall is small but comfortable, and reminds one somewhat of the Supreme Court Chamber at Washington. There are several modern paintings of historical subjects scattered through the buildings, and surrounding the hall is a series of bright and cozy committee rooms.

It is the irony of fate to find the modern Spanish Senate domiciled in the former house of Augustinian friars. Spain has changed since the days of the Inquisition, though one doubts whether the fact is recognized in America. Motley and Prescott wrote of a period covering nearly a century of Spanish greatness and Spanish cruelty; and the Spain of to-day is judged in America by that period, but the judges forget that the contemporaneous sovereigns in England were Henry VIII., Bloody Mary, and Elizabeth, with whom Ferdinand and Isabella, Charles V., and even Philip II., do not lose entirely by comparison, judged from the standpoint of cruelty.

But that is a digression, and there are features of the Spanish Senate worthy of notice, as it is a happy compromise between the English, French and American upper houses. The senators are of three classes: grandees with an annual rental from land of $10,000, sitting by right of inheritance; senators for life appointed by the crown, and lastly, senators elected by the Church, the royal academies, the universities, and each province, for the term of the Parliament. The two former classes make up one half of the House, and the elected senators the remainder. The total number of senators is three hundred and seventy-two. The House of Deputies—Congreso de los Diputados—is in a modern building begun in 1843, during the reign of Isabel II. Like the senate, it is tastefully furnished. The façade has a classical portico, and the general outline is much like the White House in Washington. There are four hundred and fifty deputies, representing the forty-nine provinces of Spain, Cuba, Puerto Rico. The Cuban delegation consists of thirty representatives, while Puerto Rico has sixteen, which is the proportion its population bears to that of the Peninsula. One curious fact in relation to the present Cortez is, that while the president of the upper house is untitled, the speaker of the Chamber, the Marquis de la Vega de Armijo, is a grandee with several titles dating back to 1679. The latter prefers the more active field of the lower house to the Senate, a seat in which he is entitled to by birth.

Among the other public buildings are the offices of the nine different ministries into which the government is divided, most of them imposing enough but modern and uninteresting. Apropos of the ministry of war, and in view of the numerous generals one reads of in connection with the Cuban war, it is amusing to note that while the peace footing of the Spanish army is about one hundred thousand men, there are

CHAMBER OF DEPUTIES

on the active list six captain-generals, thirty-nine lieutenant-generals, sixty generals of division, and one hundred and sixty brigadier-generals, making an average of one general to every three hundred and seventy soldiers. No wonder the Spanish arms have not yet proved successful. This preponderance of generals is due in part to the fact that in making peace with the Carlists the officers of the Carlist army were taken into the official fold and given their relative rank in the regular establishment. But the curse of Spain is official-dom. If two-thirds of the governmental positions could be done away with, Spain might to-day be prosperous. But the moment a butcher, baker, or candle-stick-maker acquires a competence, his son must be in the government service, in order that he may be a gentleman.

In talking of the government one is in danger of forgetting the sights of Madrid: the museums, the picture gallery, the royal armory, the palace, the royal stables, the churches, libraries, hospitals, and the hundred and one institutions which go to make up a European capital. Madrid has them all in abundance, and the tourist sees them in the hurried manner of the tourist. A description of such sights falls more within the province of a guide-book than this book of sketches, and after the last word has been written, the sights must still be seen to be appreciated. What description could do justice to the royal picture gallery in the Prado? One can say that this collection is considered the finest in the world, but that it is rather a collection of splendid gems than a complete chronological series of schools. One can say that there are sixty-two Rubens, fifty-three Teniers, ten Raphaels, forty-six Murillos, sixty-four Velasquez, twenty-two Vandykes, forty-three Titians, thirty-four Tintorettos, twenty-five Veroneses, fifty-eight Riberas, and ten Claudes hanging on the walls of that gallery, not to mention the Wouvermans, the Snyders, the Goyas, etc.; but when it has been said, what idea does it convey of that marvelous collection of paintings?

A week, a month, a year would be too short a time to study the gallery of the Prado, and yet the passing tourist rushes through its halls in a morning, or at most, in a day.

The royal armory, too, contains a unique collection of arms and armor. The nucleus was collected by Charles V. and has been added to since. The French have pilfered it as they have everything else in Spain on which they could lay their hands, and it has suffered from fire, but in spite of all, the collection is still probably the finest in the world.

Yet after all has been said the real sights of Madrid are not many. The Cook's tourist does them all in three days. Madrid is essentially a social city, and it is the people that attract one most. But not the common people as in the provinces; for in this sense there is little of the national life to be seen. The common people are merely the shop-keepers and workmen—bourgeois and ouvriers, as they are the world over. It is in the social life of Madrid that one finds much that is interesting. One meets there the governing classes of the country—the people who stand for Spain before the world. Madrid is so out of the beaten track that its society has not been flooded with foreigners. Strangers are somewhat of a rarity, and are looked on askance.

The Spaniard is reserved, and unlike the American does not throw open his arms to the foreign Tom, Dick and Harry. Even the diplomats are not social idols in Madrid as they are in Washington and Newport, and but a limited few are received into the inner circle of the smart set. But if the Spaniard knows you, and is assured that you are a reputable member of society, and above all, if he likes you, he will become the most charming of hosts, the best of friends. One has known many foreigners but none whose friendship is so warm and sincere as that of the well-bred Spaniards. But of well-bred Spaniards, as of well-bred people of every country, there is only a limited number. They are not all in the smart set, however, for a veneer of manners and mannerisms does not always make a true man. The smart set of Madrid is but a reproduction of the smart set of New York on a somewhat smaller scale. There are the same "dudes" dressed in London clothes lounging in the clubs, and the same silly women craving admiration and thirsting for excitement, the same heart-burnings, the same scandals, the same assumption of superiority to the rest of mankind, the same frittering away of time and money, with the sole difference that the people are talking pure Spanish instead of imitation English. That is, most of them are talking pure Spanish; but even in

Madrid one or two of the smartest of the
smart go to the extent of speaking
Spanish with an English accent. Anglo-
mania is not confined to Manhattan
Island. The people of this smart set are
extremely intimate and clannish, but on
the whole they are preferable to those
at home, for there is much more basis
for their pretention and much less pre-
sumption in their manner.

Spaniards do not eat and drink as
much as Anglo-Saxons and this is a point
in their favor. Dinners are not as frequent as with us except at the foreign
embassies, and those that are given are
rather informal, and among intimate
friends, and the diplomats complain
bitterly of this as a lack of hospitality.
There are of course some houses where
you dine, as you would in London, but
as a general rule the Spaniard is not
given to table hospitality. He has his
carriage, his box at the opera, his palace
always with an imposing staircase—but
last of all a French cook. To show

what a small part eating plays in the life of the Spaniard, it is only necessary to state that Madrid does not possess a single restaurant up to the French or American standard. Even at balls and receptions, the refreshments are usually of a meagre nature: some cakes, some lemonade, probably a decanter or so of sherry; but a hot supper served in courses and with unlimited champagne, would not appeal to the Spaniards, and the diplomats are left to mourn its absence, except when an embassy entertains. How the Anglo-Saxon overfeeds! It is a pity this simplicity could not be adopted elsewhere. However, one must confess that simplicity in the manner of Spanish eating is not universal.

No Spaniard is more widely known than Don Emilio Castelar, late president of the short-lived Spanish Republic, the most famous of Spanish contemporary writers, the most sincere of her statesmen; for, regardless of personal consequences, he has ever maintained a consistent course, upholding the principles he deems to be right even to the extent of alienating himself from the Republican party of his own creation, when that party began to verge toward socialism. He is a Spaniard first, last, and always, and he lives as a Spaniard, in a modest bachelor apartment, surrounded by rare art objects and the books of his choice. Being a Republican he has never put foot inside the palace, yet he has accepted the monarchy as for the best interests of Spain, but only because the monarchy has accepted religious and political liberty, the principles for which he has always struggled. Don Emilio's pride is his cuisine, but even here his patriotism reigns as in everything. His cook is Spanish, every dish which finds its way to his table is Spanish, and his wines are of the choicest Spanish vintages. One recalls a luncheon at his hospitable board, which was certainly not open to the charge of scantiness. Seventeen dishes, all Spanish, washed down with

DON EMILIO CASTELAR

the choicest of the Peninsula's wines. One cannot begin to remember the sequence of these viands, but all were unique and each had a flavor which was truly of the country. And what a charming host! How earnestly he talked, his words flowing with the rhythm of the born orator in the most sonorous of Castillian. He spoke with bitterness of the American attitude toward Cuba—his face coloring with indignation, his words emphasized with impatient gestures. "How is it possible," he asked, "that the United States can be so ungrateful to the land which gave it birth? Spain is the mother of America, and this is the base ingratitude of her child. You do not know us there. We have more liberty than England. What did we do in Spain at the time of the Republic? We declared universal suffrage, religious and political freedom, and manumitted the slaves of Cuba. All these blessings and more remain to us. It is a shame, a slander, that the people of America should call us cruel and unenlightened. Spain will fight for Cuba until the last drop of her blood is spilt; her honor demands it.'' He talked so fast and so earnestly that one could scarcely follow him, but his heart was in his words. It was a patriot speaking, a man whose soul was in his country.

But all the public men of Spain have a charming manner which some of our own politicians would do well to cultivate. Spaniards from the highest to the lowest are invariably gracious. Some of the Spanish leaders, however, affect a certain Jeffersonian simplicity which seems familiar. Don Práxedes Sagasta, for instance, the leader of the Liberal party, several times premier, Knight of the Golden Fleece, and one of the great men of Spain, lives most modestly in a second-floor apartment in the Carrera San Geronimo. Calling one afternoon with a friend, we found him in a conference with some of his political lieutenants. The impression he produces is that of a strong man who thoroughly understands the game of politics. The lines of his face are deep and well defined; he has thick, determined lips, and his shaggy gray hair and beard are almost Ibsen-esque. Rather careless in the matter of dress, and decidedly democratic in his surroundings, he has all the politeness of the true Spaniard. His manner of speaking is quiet and precise, and he seems to have the same wonderful knowledge of men and their ways which characterized the late Mr. Blaine. Señor Sagasta is an adroit political leader with a strong following and one felt, in talking with him, the forcible charm of the successful man of state. He was more guarded, too, than Castelar, and seemed less guided by sentiment; in short, more cautious.

Señor Canovas, the present prime minister, has been so much before the American public of late that he needs no mention. His clear statement of Spain's attitude in the Cuban difficulty, and his

earnest but dignified efforts to avert
hostilities should recommend him to all
Americans but jingoes. But the statesman who seems to have the most
thorough knowledge of the politics of
the world is Señor Moret y Prendergast,
deputy for Zaragoza, and minister of
foreign affairs in the late Liberal cabi-
net, a distinguished writer and an orator
of rare ability. He speaks English
fluently, and understands the Anglo-
Saxon character thoroughly, even to a
keen appreciation of the jokes in
"Puck." Señor Moret is president of
the Athenæum, a literary and artistic
club of seven hundred members, owning
an imposing building supplied with a
capital library and a large conference
hall, where from time to time distinguished speakers address the members
on political and literary subjects. On
the evening we visited the Athenæum,
Señor Silvela delivered an address on
parliamentary government. This speaker
is one of the famous men of Spain—law-

yer, writer and statesman; a conservative,
but one who is not at present in sympathy with his party leader. His de-
livery was charming. He spoke for
one hour without a single note, each
sentence perfectly rounded, each word
distinctly pronounced, and all accen-
tuated with easy, graceful gestures. His
manner in conversation was so cordial
and simple, and he seemed so pleased
with our expressions of appreciation,
that even in a few moments' chat he
gave the impression of being what the
Spaniards call "muy simpatico."

But it is impossible within the limits
of this chapter to speak of the many
interesting people you meet during a
visit to Madrid. There is a group of
Spanish writers, represented by Eche-
garay, the Spanish Ibsen, and Perez
Galdos, the novelist. They mix but
little with the social world; but Don
Juan Valera, the author of such charming stories as "Pepita Ximenez," and
"Doña Luz," is to be met occasionally

at the foreign embassies, for besides
being distinguished as a novelist and
historian, he has had a successful
diplomatic career. Señor Valera, in his
own study surrounded by his books,
seems the perfect type of the man of
letters. He has a keen interest in the
work of American writers, as he was at
one time minister at Washington. He
speaks English but little, yet his knowledge of our literature is very extended.

Progressive womanhood, too, has its
representative in Señora Emilia Pardo
Bazán, a clever and prolific novelist of
the French school, whose works have
been translated into English, and who
has a distinct place in Spanish contemporaneous literature. She stands somewhat alone, however, as the new woman
has not found her way to Spain, and
Spanish women are content to remain
in the useful sphere for which nature created them. The life of Madrid, however, centres in the Court. Men of letters are merely a side issue.

The Capital of Spain

Spain has been cursed by generations of bad kings and queens, each adding to the ruin of the country; but at last the Peninsula has a ruler who commands admiration and respect. Her Majesty Queen Maria Christina, the regent, is a true woman, dignified and tactful, and when one is presented to her he feels the force of the word queenly, that being exactly the word which describes her in manner, in figure, and in bearing.

At the private audiences occasionally granted at the request of an ambassador or minister, after passing through the antechamber and the chamber, you are ushered into the royal presence by the introducer of ambassadors. The queen receives you in a small room not unlike the reception-room of an American house. Except for the bowing low and backing out of the royal presence everything is most informal. You are invited to sit down, and permitted an interview of a few minutes. Her Majesty asks questions about various topics she thinks of interest, and then to signify that the audience is over, she rises and you retire, with numerous low bows, careful that your back is ever toward the door. Then the dapper little introducer of ambassadors, radiant in blue and gold, silk stockings and breeches, takes ·· you through a series of gorgeous rooms, where the walls are resplendent with tapestries and the portraits of Bourbons, to the apartments of the Infanta Isabel. This princess is the elder sister of the Infanta Eulalia whose name is so familiar to Americans. The latter of recent years has passed little of her time in Madrid, or even in Spain, so her elder sister is perhaps the most popular of Spanish royalties, because she is not only Spanish in her tastes, but has the marvelous faculty of never forgetting a face. Those whom the Infanta Isabel has once met she never forgets, and in the park, the opera, or wherever it is, if she sees you she greets you with a charming bow which makes one feel that he has a recognized place in her memory. She is a thorough sportswoman, too, inured to the saddle, and in the mountains around La Granja, where she passes the summer, often rides so hard that her suite are tempted to cry mercy. The Infanta Isabel receives in the same informal manner as the queen, but one feels perhaps a little more like talking freely here than in the more constraining presence of the regent.

Yet all the ceremonies of the Spanish court are not so simple. On the gala days, such as the Day of His Majesty, the twenty-third of January, the queen holds a levee, with all the ceremony the most exacting could demand. The palace of Madrid is one of the most magnificent in the world, and is in every sense a royal residence. It was built by Philip V. after the burning of the old Alcazar in 1734, with the intention of rivalling Versailles. How well this attempt succeeded may be judged by Napoleon's remarking to his brother Joseph, as the two Corsican usurpers mounted the grand staircase for the first time: "Vous serez mieux logés que moi." That lodging was but temporary and never secure, for the Spaniard is not an easy creature, even for a Napoleon, to trample on. No more imposing sight could be imagined than that grand staircase on a gala day, when it is lined with a double row of halberdiers in their Louis XIV. uniforms, and the great dignitaries of the country are ascending the steps, gorgeous in red and blue and gold and waving plumes, their breasts weighted with the glittering baubles foreigners love so well. But the deputations from the senate and the house, each preceded by four mace-bearers, form a strange contrast in their evening dress, to the glittering officials of the royal household, and it is amusing to watch the swaggering, democratic air of some of the deputies of the Left, as they stride up the stairs with a boorish attempt to show their contempt for royalty. It is customary to uncover at the first landing of the stairs, but these deputies of democratic tendencies swagger up to the door of the throne-room itself with their hats on the back of their heads, in a manner which would do credit to a Tammany politician. And this is courtly Spain. The government and the different embassies and legations enter before the others and take their places in the throne-room. Following come the provincial deputations: Ayuntamiento, the clergy, the Consejo de Estado,—or supreme court,—the Maestranzas, military orders, the officers of the army and navy, and everyone who has an official position at court. It is a brilliant kaleidoscope of gorgeousness long to be remembered.

The *damas* and *gentiles hombres*, or ladies and gentlemen in waiting, await the queen in the Ante-"Camara." The Infanta Isabel comes from her rooms to the "Camara," as do the other members of the royal family who are in Madrid.

Then the queen and the little king appear, and the court makes obeisance. The cortège is formed, the gentil hombre de servicio, the guard of halberdiers, the mayor domo de semana, the grandees, the king and queen, the Infanta Isabel, and the damas, and then the whole procession proceeds to the throne-room. There the little king, dressed on this particular occasion in the uniform of a private soldier with the collar of the Golden Fleece, to do honor to the army, sits on the right, the queen regent on his left. Standing on the dais of the throne, but behind, are the jefe superior del palacio, the mayor domo mayor, and the gentil hombre de servicio. Opposite the throne are the government and diplomatic corps, to the right the grandees, headed by the Duke of Sessa, to the left the damas, but the wives of the diplomats are gathered in an anteroom. When all are in their places, the deputation of the senate enters, and the president makes an address, to which the queen replies.

The delegation of the deputies do the same, and then all the various bodies we have seen coming up the stairs file through and make obeisance.

When all have passed, the cortège is formed as before, and the queen enters the Ante-Camara to greet the ladies of the diplomatic corps. They are standing in two lines, and the queen passes slowly by while they curtesy. She stops occasionally to speak to those she wishes particularly to favor. Then, when that ceremony is over, she passes on into the Camara and receives the private household which means the ladies' maids, the jefe de alabarderos, and the Monteros de Espinosas, a privileged corps who have the special duty of guarding the king while he sleeps. They all kiss her hand, and she then retires for a short rest before the state banquet.

None but the ministry, the grandees, the gentiles hombres, the Knights of the Golden Fleece, the president of the Consejo de Estado, the presidents of

the two chambers, the governor of the
province, the alcaide of Madrid, the archbishop of Toledo, the archbishop of Madrid, and the wives of these dignitaries,
are bidden to this feast. Formerly the
foreign ambassadors and ministers were
invited, but they have quarreled with the
grandees about precedence, and now
they are invited to a separate banquet
held in their honor. The scene, judging
by a view obtained of the banquet hall a
few moments before the arrival of the
guests, must be of unusual brilliance.
The room was ablaze with the light of
six crystal chandeliers and a hundred
silver candelabra. There was a profusion of orchids and violets and lilies of
the valley, and garlands of pink and yellow roses; there were ferns and plants,
and glass and plate in dazzling array.
The ceiling glistened with white and
gold, the walls were hung with tapestries, an army of powdered flunkeys with
coats of blue and gold and stockings of
crimson silk, awaited the coming of the

guests, and strangest of all, two tooth-
picks were arranged at each place, for
the Spaniard must pick his teeth, even in
the presence of his sovereign.

On that night a double row of servants lined the grand stairs, and halberdiers pounded the staffs of their halberds
on the stone floor as each grandee of
Spain passed up. One viewed it all
from a neighboring balcony, the glittering uniforms, the tinsel and the pomp,
and thought of another event of which
those stairs had been the scene. It was
in the early years of the troublous reign
of Queen Isabel II. Two generals,
Diego Leon, and Concha instigated by
Queen Christina, had concerted a plot
to carry off the young sovereign. Concha presented himself at the palace and
gained an entrance for himself and a
troop of soldiers by the connivance of an
officer of the outer guard who was in the
plot. There were but eighteen halberd-
iers on guard, but under their leader
Don Domingo Dulce, they advanced and

tried to parley. They were answered by bullets. A struggle ensued, the halberd-iers fighting on the stairs held their ground. Concha was repulsed. Leon arrived too late. The conspirators fled; but Leon was captured and shot for his treachery. He was young and hand-some, and the queen who heard it all too late to stay the execution, has ever kept his cross of Saint Hermergildo pierced by three bullets. It was but one of the many romances of her romantic life. The times have changed, but who can tell how soon those palace stairs may again run red with blood? The times have changed, but as long as there are kings and queens there must be palace plots and intrigues.

Spanish Society..

SPANIARDS are probably less understood in America than any people of Europe. In fact, the popular conception of the Spaniard is of a sinister scoundrel wrapped in a cloak, who smokes cigarettes and commits dark deeds—a sort of comic opera villain whose passion is cruelty. This absurdity is fully equalled by the Spanish impression of Americans—or "Los Yankees,"—as they call us. They look npon us as a species of plutocratic barbarians, whose sole merit lies in our dollars, whose manners are boorish, and whose government is the most corrupt and most overbearing in the world. It is not always pleasant to see ourselves as others see us, and when one reads in Spanish papers that the United States

is a country without principle or religion, without manliness or bravery, where
negroes are roasted alive and Italians
lynched in the public streets, where
Chinamen are persecuted and strikes are
prevalent, where anarchists are govern-
ors of states, and personal liberty is
unknown, one resents the tirade and
feels the jingo spirit surging in one's
heart.

As a matter of fact the Spanish conception of the American is merely an exaggeration of the national faults; just
as our idea of the Spaniard is a miscon-
ception of his character formed by mag-
nifying his vices at the expense of his
virtues. Human nature is much the
same the world over, and the Spaniard is
very much like other men, save that he
is down on his luck. Like most people
who have known prosperity, he finds it
difficult to appreciate his circumscribed
position, and is wont to survey himself
from the magnificent standpoint of his
former achievements.

The most pitiful person in the world, the one who most excites our sympathies, is the poor but proud aristocrat, the decayed gentleman who has seen better days, and having fallen dwells on the glories of his past instead of struggling to rise again. Spain is a nation of poor but proud aristocrats, and its government, like its people, has been struggling for years to keep up appearances, and retain the haughty position it once held in the society of nations. To retain its prominence it has been living beyond its means, and as in the case of many a patrician who has struggled to the same end, bankruptcy and ruin are the result.

If the Spaniards had had the moral courage to retire quietly from the "smart society" of nations and live within their means, they might long since have been able to regain the prominence they covet. But nations, like individuals, do not foresee disaster in time; they are carried on in the feverish current of ambition until ruined by extravagance. A

man may know his faults, may realize
his mistakes, yet lack the moral courage
to reform; he may be carried by his passions to the bittter end of destiny, realizing meanwhile the ruin which awaits
him. That is the position of Spain.
Let us pity rather than condemn.

The Spaniards are not comic opera
villains, they are a chivalrous, warm-
blooded people, having their faults as
we have ours, and their chief fault is
overweening pride. This pride is the
prevailing passion of the individual as
of the nation; it dominates society as it
does the land. Pride is so thoroughly
the ruling passion of the Spaniard
that Spanish society is to a great extent
a game of innocent deception. To keep
up appearances a Spanish family will
make any sacrifice, and the consequence
is that social life becomes an outward
show, intended to disguise financial em-
barrassment.

There are two things absolutely necessary to the maintenance of social posi-

tion in Spain, a carriage and an opera box, and it is extraordinary how much satisfaction a Spanish family derives from these luxuries. The first necessities of an Anglo-Saxon are a comfortable house and a good cook; in Spain only the very rich have either, but the display of equipages in the Retiro excels the similar show in Central Park; the opera in Madrid is as fine a sight as the opera in New York. An Anglo-Saxon invites a stranger to dine; a Spaniard takes him to drive, or to the opera. The hospitality is none the less though in a different form.

The society of a capital is always cosmopolitan. There are the diplomatic corps, the visiting foreigners, and the host of government officials to annul in a measure the national characteristics. The society of Madrid is no exception to the rule. It is cosmopolitan, but not to so great an extent as that of London or Paris. Nearly all the Spaniards of wealth live in Madrid, or visit there during a portion of the year. The city, except in the summer months, wears a holiday aspect; there is a continuous roll of carriages along the street of Alcalá and the Carrera San Geronimo; the shops are filled with French and English novelties, and the smartly dressed people who come and go wear French gowns or London made clothes. It is frequently said that Paris is not France; Madrid is certainly not Spain. The people one meets in society are of the class found in every capital. They are statesmen, soldiers, diplomats, or what are vulgarly termed "smart people." Authors, painters, and especially actors, play minor parts, for the Spaniard still regards the Bohemian in the light of an outcast.

The society of Madrid is small comparatively, but it is extremely active. The people are ever on the go, and they are intimate to a degree unknown in London. They are very clannish too, and do not receive foreigners with the open arms of a New Yorker. If Madrid were bereft of the foreign embassies and the entertainments given by the diplomats, there would be a marvelous depreciation in the gaiety of the city; but in spite of all the foreigners do, only a limited few seem to be received within the esoteric temples of the "smart set." It is interesting to note how different are the faces at an official entertainment and at a private dance, where people are invited for themselves and not for their positions; but after all the same pertains to Washington.

Dances are the joy of the Madrileñas and to their credit be it said that they dance more like Americans than any other people of Europe. They go at it with a dash and a vim not at all in keeping with their supposed dignity. The first dance one attended in Madrid was a small informal affair, with not more than fifty or sixty people present, all intimate friends. A single pianist supplied the music, and as one entered the room the familiar notes of "Daisy Bell" rolled from the keys. The people were waltzing in the American way—that is to say, reversing; they were romping too, and many of them were singing the words of the song—it seemed like home. Sometimes the levity of the Spaniards takes a childish form, as on that occasion three young swells amused themselves by purloining a couple of dozen hats belonging to the guests, which they proceeded to throw from a theatre box to a popular opera bouffe artist. The guests were left to go home in shooting caps, paper caps, mufflers, or even bareheaded, and as some of them did not relish the humor of the joke a series of duels was but narrowly averted.

The few houses where dinners are given might well be in London or Paris. The appointments are the same, the guests look, dress and talk the same, the only difference being that the gossip and scandalous stories are about different people. If one knew the people by name the same stories would be applicable, as the Madrileñas, judging by the gossip, are evidently no better or no worse than Londoners or Parisians. There is great familiarity in the use of the christian name, and men and women of all ages call each other Pepita, Carmen, Maria, Pepe, Gonzalo, or whatever their prenomens may be, with an intimacy scarcely equalled in our American country towns.

A society will be dazzling, witty or corrupt, according to the beauty, intelligence and morality of its women. Judged by this standard the society of Madrid, though one hesitates to say it boldly, appears somewhat mediocre. The women of Spain are often extremely beautiful, but it is among the lower classes rather than the upper, that real beauty is most often found. A Spanish woman reaches her prime at fifteen or sixteen, but she ages quickly, and usually develops a tendency to corpulency. Her education is not of a character tending to

develop her mental powers. She is
brought up to be a wife and a mother,
and her studies are of the most rudimen-
tary nature. In religion, however, her
instruction is most careful, but she is not
permitted to think for herself. The
priest is the supreme guardian of her
conscience, and she is so thoroughly
grounded in the tenets of Romanism that
she usually becomes a devotionist. The
Spanish women have delightful manners;
they are thoroughly feminine and charming, but they read very little, and seem
quite incapable of discussing the affairs
of the world as do their Anglo-Saxon
sisters. The women of Madrid, however, seem to be deeply interested in
court intrigue and are violent political
partisans; but the new woman is an unknown quantity, and such societies as
the Sorosis are undreamt of.

Of home life among the Spaniards, there
seems to be quite as much as, if not more
than, with us. The family ties are very
strong, and there is more parental rever-

ence than among Americans. The Spanish families are perhaps more comparable to the French, with this exception: filial love and parental affection are not the all-absorbing passions. Spanish young men and girls are permitted more latitude in the matter of love-making than the French, though they are hampered by conventionalities unknown in Saxon lands. Love matches are common, but the lovers are not allowed the privilege of seclusion from the eyes of the world. They meet at the theatre, at dances, in the park, or wherever society congregates, but they must be ever under the eye of a dueña. The wishes of contracting parties to marriages are, however, more generally consulted than in France, and engagements are frequently of very long duration. Spanish girls are rather sentimental in their ideas of love. Marriage is a favorite topic of their conversation. It is the one event of their lives, to which they look forward for it means to a great extent emancipation.

But the married women do not have the liberty of American wives; they must be much more guarded in their actions, and the husband is the ruler of the household. Spaniards say that the liberty accorded American women would be impossible in Spain—the blood flows too warmly there—scandal would surely ensue.

The traditions of Spain are all monarchical; the nobility have great power and influence, and the possession of a title is almost a *sine qua non* of social distinction. The Spanish nobility is more comparable to that of England than to the nobility of other European countries, but it has a distinctive feature of its own in the "Grandees of Spain." Grandees are nobles to whom special hereditary privileges have been granted. Those having an annual rental from land of $10,000 sit in the senate, and all grandees have the curious privilege of remaining covered in the presence of the sovereign. As "cousins" of the king

HIS MAJESTY ALFONSO XIII

they take precedence of the diplomatic corps, but this ·has given rise to such vigorous protest on the part of the diplomats that separate state banquets are given for the ambassadors and the grandees. A grandee in uniform wears a gold key over the right hip, as a sign that he may enter the palace and confer with his sovereign at any time. It is his most cherished privilege, and one which the monarch is bound to regard. When a grandee passes a palace guard, he is saluted by a sharp pound of the halberd upon the marble floor. These special privileges date from the reign of the emperor Charles V. who created twelve grandees. The number, having been increased by successive monarchs, is now much larger, although but a small portion of the nobility are grandees. The privileges of grandees are confined to the higher nobility, as none of the viscounts or barons are grandees (except in the case of the Duke of Infantado, who has two baronial titles with gran-

deza privileges), and but one in ten of
the thousand marquises, and seven hundred odd counts wear the coveted gold-
en key; while all of the hundred and
nine ducal titles carry with them the
privileges and honors of a Grandee of
Spain. Spanish titles, like the English,
descend to the eldest son, and the heir
to a grandeeship has no especial appella-
tion beyond that of excellency. The
Spaniards regard their nobility as second
to none in lineage, but although a few
of the titles date to the early part of the
fifteenth century, and one or two to the
fourteenth, it is nevertheless a fact that
about one-third of the Spanish titles
have been created in the present century.

There is a curious fact in relation to
Spanish titles which may be of great interest to unmarried American millionaires anxious to emulate the example set
by our heiresses. Titles not only descend through the female line, but a
man upon marrying a titled woman immediately assumes his wife's title. There

is at least one unmarried duchess in Spain and several marchionesses. An American upon marrying a duchess would be created a duke and a grandee, and by purchasing a property with an annual rental of ten thousand dollars would have a seat for life in the senate—what an opportunity for some New Yorker.

There is probably no court in Europe where there is more etiquette than at the court of Spain. To an American who views the bowings and scrapings, and endless red tape, it all seems such a waste of valuable time, such a sham and mockery, that republican institutions, in spite of their faults, stand out in honorable contrast. Yet a monarchy is suited to the Spanish character. One doubts if a republic could thrive among a people so proud, so excitable, and withal, so ignorant.

Spaniards are not what Dr. Johnson termed "clubable" men; they have their clubs, but in most instances they are like those of France, that is to say, gambling houses, with restricted membership. Roulette and baccarat flourish, and the place most frequented is the gaming-room. However, the most exclusive club in Madrid does not permit games of chance. In the matter of buildings, the clubs of Madrid are inferior to those of the provinces, as the pride of a provincial city is its casino, or club. In Cordova, for instance, the casino is a most elaborate affair, covering a large area, and supplied with accommodations ample for a city of twice the size. In Seville, too, there are several clubs in the Sierpes with creditable buildings, while the most exclusive club in Madrid occupies a small portion of an apartment house, and is in no way remarkable for its equipment. There are a few large clubs in the capital, with handsome buildings, but the membership of such institutions is selected rather casually, and the social standing is not high. There is a "Fine Arts" club, composed principally of artists and literary men, and several military casinos, but only one club in Madrid seemed at all comparable to the best clubs of London, Paris or New York. It is frequented by the most fashionable young men and the best known diplomats. But it was in no way Spanish; in fact French and English were spoken there more frequently than the language of the country. Another club is more thoroughly typical of the country. It is fashionable to a great extent, but there is a free and easy air about the place which is rather refreshing. Strange caricatures of the prominent members have been drawn upon the walls, and the habitués seem thoroughly at home. It also occupies but a portion of an apartment building, but there is much originality in the decoration and furnishing of the rooms. Unfortunately gambling is permitted and the green tables are surrounded by flushed and anxious faces.

As has been said, Madrid is not Spain.

In the provinces society is typical of the country; it is more dignified, and necessarily more dull. The provincial nobility are abnormally proud, and it is in the smaller cities that one meets Spaniards whose bearing is that of the hidalgo of romance. In Seville, for instance, the third city of Spain, and socially the second, there is a dullness in the social life that is apparent even to the casual visitor. The people drive in state in the afternoon, they go to the opera night after night, but that is all. On fête days they visit each other, but dances and dinners are so rare that a supper party given during the time of one's visit was discussed with the interest that a state ball would have created in Madrid. In the provinces, too, the desire to keep up appearances is more noticeable. People economize in the household expenses to the smallest item, in order that their names may appear among the box holders at the opera. It is even said that the women driving in the park are sometimes fashionably dressed above the waist, while a carriage-rug covers well-worn apparel. Such stories are told by Spaniards themselves; their reliability one does not vouch for, but one cannot fail to notice the elaborate excuses offered for not extending dinner invitations. But withal there are no people more courteous and hospitable than the Spaniards. They will go to infinite pains to pay the smallest attention to a stranger; will even tramp from church to church, and gallery to gallery, in endeavoring to show one the sights; they will take you shopping, call at your hotel twice a day to offer their services, and in short, do a thousand and one things no Anglo-Saxon would ever dream of.

The Spaniard may be overweening in his pride, but he is overpowering in his courtesy. An Englishman or an American will dismiss a stranger with a dinner, and feel that he has done his duty; a Spaniard will avoid giving such an invitation by every possible excuse, because his pride prevents his extending hospitality for which his means are inadequate; but he will send you flowers and take you to drive each day of your visit; he will bestow countless little attentions, and show a real interest in your welfare, and a desire to please, which make you feel that his hospitality is not perfunctory. When you part from him you feel that you have parted from a friend. There are little courtesies of ordinary occurrence in Spain which contrast forcibly with Anglo-Saxon boorishness. For instance, no one enters a railway carriage without bowing to every occupant, and on leaving the same ceremony is gone through with. On taking one's seat at a hotel table it is customary to salute each of the guests, and on leaving one does the same. Upon entering a shop you greet the shopkeeper, and when leaving "God be with you," or "May all be well with you," are the words he utters, even if you have failed

PLAZA DE TOROS, MADRID

to make a purchase. It is only in commercial Barcelona that anything comparable to incivility is apparent, and Barcelona is the home of socialism and anarchy; its society is composed of the class of people the French call the bourgeoisie.

The Spaniard is proud and apathetic to a degree, but he has commendable qualities as well. It is difficult to excuse him to Americans because his characteristics are the reverse of those most universally admired in this country. He is not a ''hustler'' nor a money getter, and he is open to the charge of cruelty in his national sport; but even that is a matter of education. One remembers distinctly a young Spanish officer who had just witnessed a Yale-Princeton football game, saying that he considered the sport barbarous and cruel, and totally unfit for gentlemen. That same man was an ardent ''aficionado'' of bull-fighting.

There are no more enthusiastic patrons

of the bull-ring in Madrid than many of
the foreign diplomats, and one remembers clearly the secretary of the United
States legation stationed in Madrid at
the time of a former visit, saying that
he was an annual subscriber and had
not missed a "Corrida" during his entire
term of office.   After all the Spaniard is
what heaven has created him — a proud,
sensitive and courteous creature, sincere
in his fidelity to his church, his country,
and his family; insincere perhaps in his
dealings with others; cruel as we understand cruelty, indolent too; but nevertheless an average man, who has suffered
much in the school of adversity, and
whose future depends upon his ability to
profit by the lessons of the past.

Seville the Fair.

FAIR and delicate as a maiden, a city for delightful fancies, where fountains trickle in shady courts and oranges bloom, where the sun is ever shining and the lover ever whispering at the lattice of his mistress. That is Seville, the gem of Andalusia, and Andalusia means all that is fairest in Spain. It is a city where white-walled houses with hanging balconies and sloping roofs are scattered gracefully about in bewildering streets and lanes, with no more apparent purpose than to be picturesque.

There are brilliant highways, where the roll of carriages is heard and the mules of tram cars clatter over the stones. There are sleepy byways too, with rows of dingy little shops, where artisans are working and their wares are

displayed for sale, while mingled with
the hovels of the poor are the imposing
entrances of patrician houses where the
passer-by peers enviously through courts
with growing palms and marble columns
glistening in the sunlight.

He who has not seen Seville has not
seen a marvel (Quien no ha visto Sevilla
no ha visto maravilla) runs an Andalusian
proverb, but there is nothing marvelous
in Seville. It is dainty and graceful
with the delicacy of a piece of old lace,
or a rare bit of Dresden. Wherever one
turns there is color and beauty and grace
in outline; nothing seems inharmonious
unless it be the beggars, and even they
are picturesque. Only the cathedral, rising massive and grand in the centre of
the city, recalls the vicissitudes of history, and makes one remember that the
Phœnician and the Roman, the Visigoth
and Moor were each in turn masters of
Seville before the fires of the Inquisition
blazed in the public squares, or the
tramp of Napoleon's soldiers echoed

through the streets. On the site of this cathedral a pagan temple and a Gothic basilica, a Moorish mosque and another Christian church have stood, and now in the splendid pile of to-day the Moorish and the Gothic, the Græco-Roman and the plateresque are blended, each in the zenith of its strength.

This ponderous church stands sombre and grey among the delicate houses of Seville like an altar of death in the midst of revelry. It is mighty and magnificent, yet so unlike the gay cheerful city, that one pauses to wonder whence it came. Only the beautiful Giralda, with its slender belfry and graceful Moorish arches rising against the pale blue sky seems to be of Seville; the rest is solemn, one might even say repulsive, were it not for its grandeur. Yet one pauses to admire the splendid Gothic portals with their sculptured saints and patriarchs, or the light flying buttresses which spring from nave to nave with the profusion of pinnacles and domes above.

Only when one enters does one appreciate the harmony and unity of that edifice. Other churches are chaste and
magnificent, and even grand, but the first
impression of the cathedral of Seville is
one of solemn reverence. There is a
severity and simplicity in those vast proportions which is awe-inspiring, and
wandering through the lofty nave and
splendid chapels, with their gorgeous
gilt retablos and priceless works of art,
where sombre figures kneel in prayer, and
the chanting of priests echoes from the
walls, where candles glimmer and the
odor of incense fills the air, one knows
that it is the House of God. But that
is the impression of another visit. Part
of the roof fell in some ten years since,
and now huge scaffolding fills in the
greater portion of the church, and the
click of hammer and chisel is heard.
The work of restoration seems nearly
complete, but the slowness of Spanish
labor is such that four years must elapse
before the scaffolding can be removed.

Seville the Fair

This cathedral has its quota of the bones of saints and pieces of the true cross; there are jewels and gold embroidered vestments, the tombs of kings and the mistresses of kings, and noble paintings by the master hand of Murillo; but churches grow gloomy and cold, and sunlight fills the streets of Seville.

There is an old friend outside, one you cannot exactly recall, but whose form seems familiar. It is the Moorish Giralda, once a watch tower, but now the belfry of the cathedral. Somehow your thoughts turn towards America and you think of Madison Square, and the Garden tower, and then you see a family likeness in towers, not one that is objectionable, however, or in the least discreditable, for what grander inspiration could an artist have than this tower of Seville?

The bells above are clanging the hour of vespers, and slowly climbing the gentle incline which leads round and round within the Giralda walls, you reach the top in time to see the setting of the sun. Below are the moss-grown domes and countless pinnacles of the cathedral, and then the white-walled houses of the city, with their quaint tile roofs, lie in confusion as though some child had overturned a box of play houses and left them there as they had fallen. No streets are visible except directly below, for the streets are so narrow and irregular as to be lost in the jumble of walls and roofs; but rising above the tiles and whitewash are the sombre belfries of churches, the Plaza de Toros, the huge square tobacco factory, and the Alcazar with its red Moorish towers, and gardens where the cyprus and orange grow, and slender palms are scattered in profusion. Then the Guadalquivir winds like a silver serpent past the wooded promenade they call "Las Delicias," and the Torre del Oro now truly golden in the fading sunlight. Across the river, with its shipping and its graceful bridges, lies Triana, the suburb of gypsies and porcelain factories, where

Trajan is said to have been born, and the worst spirits of the city congregate, and beyond all, the green plain of Seville rolls towards Cadiz and the sea, dotted here and there with olive groves and white pueblos. To the west, towards the ancient port of Palos, the sun is setting behind the foothills of the Sierra Morena. The floating clouds above are golden, the river glistens, deep shadows fall upon the plain, and then, as the crimson sun sinks behind the line of purple hills, the night creeps chilly and dark across the Vega. The bells above cease clanging, the noises of the streets grow still, lights twinkle here and there and everywhere, and in the court below the black-robed priests come and go in the twilight like spirits of the dead. One might dream there forever, but the blind guardian of the tower jingles his bunch of keys impatiently; the hour for closing has arrived. Then you grope your way to the earth again and stroll through the town. The little shops are lighted, the narrow streets are crowded, for it is the time of the evening promenade, when all Seville turns out to wander through the Sierpes; all Seville wrapped in its capa or its mantilla.

The Sierpes is a curious street, or lane, or whatever it be, for it is narrow and crooked, and it is closed to carriages. The clubs and cafés are there, and the fashionable shops. People saunter there in the daytime and they saunter there at night. They lounge in the windows of the clubs, and sip black coffee at the marble tables of the cafés, or they stroll to and fro gazing at the trinkets from Paris and London displayed in the shops. Spaniards are never in a hurry. There is a charming lack of energy about them which, from an artistic standpoint, is delightful. A man in a hurry is never picturesque, whatever else he may be, and to one accustomed to the bustling streets of America it is a real pleasure to mingle with a sauntering Spanish crowd and watch the apparent indiffer-

THE BURERO

ence with which they treat the affairs of the world.   From the grand señor to the beggar they walk with the same loitering step, their graceful capas thrown about their shoulders, their broad brimmed hats poised easily upon their heads, a cigarillo ever burning between their lips. And the olive-skinned women, so beautiful, but alas! so fat, amble by like palfreys, and look at one with their dark, soulful eyes, coquettishly perhaps, or more often scornful.

But if you want to see lithe, quick movements, you must drop into the "Burero" and watch the dancing girls as they dance the "baile flamenco" to the twanging of guitars and the clapping of hands.   It is the resort of the people, where crowds sit at the rough wooden tables and sip their copas of manzanilla, or aguardiente.   From the gallery above you look down upon the stage and the people.   It is like a picture by Fortuny.   Such strong effects of lights and shadows — such brilliant colors;   there are the bright shawls of the women, the sashes of the men, the uniforms of the soldiers; the walls are striped in blue and yellow, and the lights shine dimly through the smoke. The dark faces are so brutish, and the scene so Spanish, you wish you were an artist and could paint it all. Otero, the Parisian favorite, began her career in such a place, and the girl who is dancing (Lorlita they call her), a lithe, young creature, slender and beautiful, with the dark languishing beauty of the south, perhaps she will have princes and American millionaires at her feet some day. She is worthy of it, if such creatures ever are. Her eyes glisten in the light of lamps, a crimson rose is in her hair. "Eh, Lorlita! niña!" shout the other dancing girls, who sit upon the stage clapping their hands, as with stamping feet and snapping fingers, her head thrown back imperiously, her body writhing like a serpent, she dances the dance of the Gitanas, with the sensuous abandon of her race. Three impassive Spaniards, with bloated faces and little beastly eyes, twang their guitars; one of them sings in a high-pitched key a quaint accompanying refrain with words not always the purest, while, strangest of all, a group of children, offspring of the dancing girls, play in the room behind the stage. As Lorlita, the favorite, finishes her wild dance, a storm of applause breaks forth, men get upon the benches and shout, a dozen or more hats are thrown upon the stage. That is the Burero, but in time it palls, for the other girls are plain and fat, and the air is not of the best.

Wandering home through the dark winding byways, you pass cloaked figures whispering at iron-barred windows. They are the lovers of Seville, *pelando la pava* (plucking the turkey), as they call it. With the lattice slightly open the fair Sevilliana sits in her darkened chamber talking in whispered tones to the gallant without. The "old folks," to borrow a homely phrase, being weary of the task of chaperonage, after locking the daughter in a room barred like a prison cell, have gone to bed, and for hours, sometimes the entire night, the affianced lovers look through the grating into each others' eyes, and whisper the nothings of love. It would seem cold comfort to a northern swain, but the Spaniards say the iron bars are a necessary evil there in the south where the blood runs warm.

In the early morning, when the air is chilly and streets are still in shadow, you loiter towards the market; that is, if you are fond of life and character. The market of Seville, like the people, is picturesque. The old stone arcade, which forms a quadrangle about the booths, has a charm which is quaint and Spanish. Its walls rise white against the blue sky, and deep shadows of its graceful arches are cast upon the flagstones. The striped awnings of the stalls blend with the multi-colored shawls of the market women; piles of oranges and lemons

glisten in the sunlight; there are festoons
of grapes, and strings of garlic dangling
from the arches; citrons and grape fruit
hang in hempen slings, while apples and
radishes, onions and cabbages, lie heaped
in artistic confusion upon the pavement.
The hum of voices, the shrill cries of
venders fill the air, but the people loiter
and gossip, and sun themselves. No one
is in a hurry. Old stooping men in
capas slink among the crowded market
stalls, puffing the ever present cigarillo;
olive-skinned women in faded cotton
gowns and brilliant colored shawls waddle along with babes and baskets in their
arms, or stop to prattle and bargain with
the fat and greasy butchers, who stand
enshrined like sacrificial priests behind
their altars of beef and mutton and
their bowers of sausages. Blue smocked
porters with cords and mantas slung
across their shoulders lounge in the sunlight. Pretty girls, with roses in their
hair and roguish eyes, flirt with the
slender, black-haired youths who loiter

in groups; the dogs bark, the children
play, but they play in the listless, lazy
way of Spain. There is life and color
everywhere, and you think the Spaniard
was born to be an artist's model, for
Seville is the painters' paradise.

But in the maze of tortuous streets
about the market one sees more of the life
of the people. There the whitewashed
houses are outlined against the brilliant
sky in rambling perspective, and the
graceful tower of some parish church,
its brown walls moss grown, its bright
tiles shining, rises sharp and clear into the
blue above. Dark maidens, with glossy
hair and warm color in their cheeks,
gaze idly from the miradores above
upon the countless people in the narrow street below. The cobbler ham-
mers and stitches in his smoky little shop
without window or door, glasses clink in
the taberna, sleek cows with mournful
eyes and tinkling bells stand silently
chewing their cuds in the milkman's
stall, and the dainty feet of shaggy don-

keys patter on the cobble stones, as the patient little beasts thread their way through the street, only their huge swaying ears and little tails visible beneath their bulging panniers of straw or charcoal. Then you wander along, picking your way through the good-natured crowds until you reach some little plaza, with its quaint parish church where beggars sun themselves upon the flagstones, and the puestos, or booths of street peddlers, with graceful colored awnings are scattered picturesquely about the pavement. There the dazzling sunlight casts fantastic shadows on the yellow and blue walls of the houses, multi-colored pots, or festoons of cotton prints hang in the dingy shops, gallardos—dandies of the street—gossip in groups, or ogle the passing maidens; dogs snooze in sunny spots, and crowds of idlers cluster about some barrel organ or blind guitarist. There is a booth near by where a bronze-skinned gipsy is cooking *molletes calentitos*, a sort of greasy flour cake fried in oil, and a wine puesto with its earthen jars and huge bottles of red and yellow wine, and there vagos loiter to eat and drink.

One can stroll for hours in the streets of Seville, watching the people and talking with them, too, for the Andalusian of the lower classes is the best of fellows. There is a democratic freedom in his manner, at once respectful and cordial, which is unlike the obsequiousness or the boorishness of the common people of other countries. He is slow and even lazy, but he commands respect, and nowhere can one meet such civility and heartiness as is shown by the Andalusian peasant. But you must unbend and meet him half way. He does not like Saxon stiffness, and a cordial word or the offer of a cigarette will accomplish more than a handful of silver. When you go into a taberna of the people where aguardiente and manzanilla are sold at a cent a glass, the habitues all greet you with a word of welcome, and the barkeeper serves his liquor with a courtliness which is Chesterfieldian.

They are rough places, those common taverns. There is one in particular, across the river in Triana, where the "Bowery toughs" of Seville, the *matones* they are called, gather to drink and quarrel. They say that every Sevillian who is spoiling for a fight goes there, and many are the cutting affrays when *navajos* are drawn, and with mantas wrapped about the left arm, the duellists crouch and slowly follow each other around watching the opportunity for the fatal spring, just as they do in Carmen. This taberna of the bullies is a low dingy place, spanned by high beams smoked black by ages of cigarettes and dirt. It is open to the street on two sides, and supporting the corner beams is an old Roman column which looks as though it may have been standing since the time of Trajan. The floor is of dirt, and in one corner is a low table and three or four well-worn cane-seat chairs.

There are dirty bottles on the shelves and coarse prints of bull fighters hang upon the walls, while behind the bar is the keeper of the resort, a low browed ruffian, with little weazel eyes set close together, and a knife slash across his unshaven cheek. He looks a prince of cut-throats, but even he has a kindly greeting, and a civil word, as do the group of "sports" who lean upon the bar. Those "toughs" of Seville are not unlike their Bowery prototypes. They have the same hangdog features and swaggering manner, and their heads hang forward and their elbows are thrown out as they are in New York. Their hats are tipped over their eyes too, and were it not for the short braided jackets and the gaudy sashes, the tight corduroy trousers, and the array of coster-like buttons, one might expect to hear them exclaim, in the language of Chimmie Fadden, "What t' ell."

But the Sevillian of a more respectable class is more entertaining. The honest workman, out for a holiday with his best girl, or the bourgeois and his friends picnicking in the environs under the shade of olive tree—these true Andalusians will always welcome a stranger; they will share their sour wine and sweet cakes, and the bright-eyed girls of the party will dance the graceful Sevillana to the time of castanets, and if you speak Spanish you may chat with them all, and feel when you leave that you have met real friends.   No, there are no people as friendly and witty and gracious as the Andalusians.   And all that reminds one that perhaps the most delightful of Sevillian days are those when one takes a carriage and drives into the country, say to Italica, where there are the ruins of a Roman amphitheatre.

The horses are harnessed in the Andalusian fashion, with jangling bells and streaming ribbons; the little driver sits erect upon his box, his broad brimmed hat a-tilt, not a crease in his short Andalusian jacket.   Over the hard, tree-lined

road the tough little beasts scamper,
and you lean back against the cushion,
and breathe in the perfect air. And
what a succession of charming scenes.
Quaint villages of a single street, and
houses of a single story, the walls of white-
washed stone, or mud and brick, thatched
with faggots, with cool shady porches
where skinny men doze in low chairs, and
sunny spots where groups of loafers are
playing cards. Women are washing in the
streams, strings of donkeys come and go,
their little backs bending under the
weight of panniers of pottery; meek
horses amble by bearing a man astride
and a woman sidewise; goats, pigs, gypsy
girls dancing by the wayside; soldiers,
beggars, a drunkard sleeping in the sun,
and beyond it all the green rolling fields
tufted with brown olive trees, the silvery
river, and graceful Seville outlined against
the blue sky, with her Giralda and her
fifty church towers, her lanky chimneys
and her shining walls of white.

Before you know it an hour has

passed, and you have reached the amphi-theatre. It is like other ruins of the kind, grey rocks crumbling and moss-grown, rising in tiers of seats, with the arena and the cages for the beasts below. Donkeys browse upon the hill-side, peasants bask in the sun and in the shade, just under the walls of what may have been the podium where the Roman magistrates sat, a party of picnickers are dancing the Sevillana to the time of castanet and tambourine, and the echo of the accompanying song swells across the amphitheatre. Some of the men come forward to offer glasses of manzanilla, and exchange the day's greetings. It is not a tip they are after; to offer one would be an insult; they are prompted purely by the spirit of goodfel-lowship. You laugh and talk with them and exchange a cigarillo for the drink, and then picking some wayside flowers you offer them to the girls. They smile and show their pretty teeth, and dance again, not the vulgar flamenco or tango, but the charming dance of the province, with its agile movements and graceful poses. It is hard to realize that in that peaceful arena some two thousand years ago, wild beasts fought and the blood of gladiators stained the sand.

That is one of the excursions into the country, and there are many others. The daily drive, however, is to Las Delicias, the tree-lined promenade along the river bank, where society turns out in French built carriages and gazes enviously at each other for an hour or so each afternoon. Driving along the river front, with its stone quays and railways, its shipping and its stevedores, one passes the orange-colored Torre del Oro (Tower of Gold), where the Moors stood guard, and Peter the Cruel confined his fallen favorites, and then on the left the red palace of San Telmo, with its delightful gardens of oranges and citrons, palms and tropical plants, where the Infanta Maria Luisa lives. This princess is mother of the Countess

of Paris, and of Don Antonio, who fig-
ured in America as the husband of the
Infanta Eulalia. She is better known,
perhaps, as the widowed Duchess of
Montpensier. Her life is quiet enough
now, but it must have been different when
her husband was alive, for he was the
arch intriguer, only excelled by his
mother-in-law, Maria Christina, the
queen of Ferdinand Seventh, and
mother of Isabella Second. But if one
begins talking of the palace intriguers
in the age of the Camarillas there will
be no end. This widowed duchess, and
old Queen Isabella, living away off in
Paris, are about all that are left from
the disgraceful days of Espartero and
O'Donnell, Serrano and Marvaez, when
palace favorites were overturning ministries at will, and the country was going
to the dogs. The government of to-day
has much to learn, but the improvement
that some twenty years have brought is
marvelous.

But to return to the palace of San

Telmo.   It marks the beginning of Las
Delicias, and there the "quality" of
Seville drive, ride and walk.   Las Delicias is not a park; it is merely a long
straight drive, skirted by gardens and
villas on the one hand, by the river and
a narrow strip of land, laid out with
trees and walks, upon the other.   There
is but little of the national life to be seen
there; mostly Parisian bonnets and
Parisian gowns, artificial complexions
and artificial smiles, a very minute pro-
duction of the Bois.   But occasionally
a family of the older Spanish school rum-
bles by, their lumbering coach drawn by
mules, their dark Spanish faces adorned
with mantillas; the mother fat and
greasy, the daughters slim and demure,
and all with incipient mustaches.   There
are the four-in-hands from the country,
too, with jangling bells, gaily padded
collars and bobbing tassels on the
bridles, which roll through the drive at a
swinging gait, and some of the splendid
saddle-horses, with their arched necks and

well turned limbs, are ridden in Andalusian style, with light padded saddles and Moorish stirrups, and the bridle ornamented by a network of braided tassels. The men who ride them are Spanish too, with their broad brimmed hats and smart braided jackets, and perhaps you meet a high break with a load of bull fighters, their hair braided in short cues, or some women of rapid tendencies, dressed à la bolera, and driving a trap in Spanish style; but most of the carriages are those of Paris, and there is a sprinkling of smart hussars and gunners, in their uniforms of blue and gold.

But the society of Seville is provincial and dull; there are very few balls, and dinners, except amongst intimate friends in a quiet way, are almost unknown; in fact, but few houses possess the necessary paraphernalia for the giving of a dinner, and in the event of such an entertainment being necessary, the resources of the Hotel de Madrid are called into service. The Sevillians drive in the park, and they go to the opera; they visit each other on feast days, and they call after a death in the family; but they have very little of the social life which characterizes an American city, or even Madrid. The nobility of the provinces are intensely proud, so they live with a great deal of outward pretense; their carriages are superb, they have enormous palaces, with numerous liveried flunkies to usher one in; they all have their boxes at the opera, but they live most simply. The last extravagance in which an American indulges is an opera box, it is the first necessity of a Sevillian; the conditions of life are reversed. To a stranger the Sevillian nobleman is very courteous, he invites you to drive in the park, he takes you to his club and to his box at the opera, he sends you flowers, but a dinner, that universal courtesy of the Anglo-Saxon, is not forthcoming until you know him extremely well, and then you dine en famille. Once only during the year does the society of Seville throw aside its sombre aspect and indulge in frivolity. That is during Holy Week and the fair which follows. Then Seville is *en fête*, the society of Madrid are its guests, and people flock there from all of Spain and Europe. There is a round of entertainments, the ladies of Seville have booths at the fair for the amusement of their friends, they even assume the national costumes and dance the national dances; but when it is over they drop back to their prosaic life with its daily drive in Las Delicias.

The houses of the nobility of Seville are veritable palaces. They are all built on much the same plan. There is a cool, delightful patio, or central court open to the blue sky and sunlight, with marble columns and Moorish arches, playing fountains and groups of palms and foliage plants. Divans, easy chairs, and rugs are scattered about invitingly, and during the hot summer days the family live there mostly, and sleep in the lower rooms away from the heat, while in winter they retire to the floor above. The staircase is always imposing. The steps are of marble, and the walls of shining tiles, while the family arms are usually emblazoned on the ceiling. There are but two stories, and on the floor above, surrounding the court, or series of courts, for there are often several, are the drawing room with its satin and gold furniture, the library, the dining room, with carved oak wainscoting and high back chairs, the family chapel, with its little altar and its cushioned prie-dieu, its pictures of saints and burning candles, and then the sleeping rooms of the family and domestic offices. Some of these houses possess rare art treasures, and walking about with the host, it is no unusual thing to have him call attention in a careless way to some rare Murillo or Van Dyke.

All this, however, is of the town and people. One forgets the glorious monu-

THE ALCAZAR

ments of Seville, the scores of churches, the picture gallery, where are many of Murillo's masterpieces, the plateresque Town Hall from the time of Charles V., rich in medallions, pilasters, archivaults, and friezes of superb design; the Casa de Pilatus, the Lonja; the huge tobacco factory, where five thousand ugly, dirty women, vaunted as beautiful, roll cigars and cigarettes and nurse their sickly babies. All these and many others are the sights of Seville, where crowds of tourists flock to gape and wonder. Each, perhaps, is worthy of a chapter by itself, of the guide book sort, with dates and details; but one who loves the picturesque cares more for the people and the streets, the donkeys and the beggars.

There is one monument, however, which is unique. It is the Moorish Alcazar, with its castellated walls, red and moss-grown, its portal blazoned with the arms of Castile and Leon, replete with historical memories of the Moorish kings of Seville; Saint Ferdinand, the conqueror; Peter, "the Cruel" or "the Just," according to one's sympathies; and Maria de Padilla, his dark-eyed mistress. There one can wander by the hour through the maze of Moorish rooms, gorgeous with ivory and gold, brilliant with color. The palace has been restored and one sees the Moorish architecture glittering and vivid as it was in former days. The repairs have been done in a paltry manner, however, and paint too often takes the place of porcelain, but the palace with its pillarets of precious marble, its arches and azulejos, its stalactite ceilings and intricate stucco work, delicate as a pattern of finest lace, is beautiful and splendid. When the sunlight streams through the miradores there is a dazzling profusion of color; green, red, brown and gold, but one prefers the delicate Alhambra, where time has faded the colors and the harsh hand of the restorer has left the walls untouched.

It is in the charming gardens of the

Alcazar that one tarries longest. There the orange and the citron grow and the air is sweet with the odor of flowers; the sunlight casts cool shadows upon the moss-grown pavements and the stuccoed walls; while surrounding one in maze-like confusion are close-cropped hedges of myrtle, and cypresses cut in fantastic forms. There are magnolias and sweet lemons, and the towering forms of graceful palms; there are Moorish kiosks and moss-grown fountains where water trickles from the mouths of lions and gold fish glitter. The air is balmy and soft, and soothed by the gentle stirring of the leaves, one dreams the hours away, thinking of Seville the Fair, and its departed glory—of the days of Peter and Charles the Great, when cavaliers and courtiers wandered in those gardens and the laughter of dark-eyed favorites echoed through the leaves.

Spanish Sports.

IT is impossible to defend the national sport of Spain. Undeniably cruel, it is at the same time fascinating, exciting and alluring; in short, the finest spectacle of modern days, comparable only to gladiatorial shows of ancient Rome. The sandy arena, with its array of glittering toreadors, the tier upon tier of seats, crowded with excited faces; the beautiful women with their graceful white mantillas; the uniforms of soldiers, the glaring sunlight, the blue canopy of sky above the amphitheatre, combine in forming a picture never to be forgotten. The tragedy, too, where the skill and daring of man is matched against the most ferocious brute in the world, fascinates while it disgusts, and appeals in quick succession to one's pity, anger and inborn love of contest.

A TOREADOR

Spanish Sports

While condemning the sport from the moralist's standpoint, it is easy to understand its hold upon the populace. A liberal Spaniard once said to the writer that so long as there were priests and bull-fights in Spain, the country could not progress. There is much truth in the remark, although generalizations are usually too sweeping. However, so far as bull-fights are concerned, the country would unquestionably be better without them. But from the picturesque standpoint Spain without *corridas de toros* would not be Spain.

No country in the world has a national sport so typical or so thoroughly a part of the national life. Yet, like American base-ball, bull-fighting has degenerated. It is no longer a sport for gentlemen alone, but a hippodrome performance in which the actors are hired ruffians. In that, too, it resembles the gladiatorial sports of Rome; but although Hispania Romana was the most Roman of all the provinces, and the Spaniard is the most Latin of modern Europeans, it is questionable whether bull-fighting has any connection with the sports of Rome beyond an undoubted similarity.

On the contrary there is much evidence to prove that *corridas de toros* were unknown in Spain until the coming of the Moors. Suetonius, Pliny and other Latin writers who described in detail Spanish games in the arena, make no mention of combats between bulls and men, and most authorities agree in stating that bull-baiting is a survival of the African and Moorish custom of hunting live boars. There is frequent mention in the early Spanish chronicles of the public baiting of *cerdos*, and with the spread of agriculture, the bull undoubtedly formed a more accessible and more formidable adversary. But if bull-fighting is not of Roman origin it is decidedly of Roman character, and the Spanish people, for centuries the most Latin of Roman provincials, still possess enough of Roman character to take kindly to a sport so thoroughly, in sentiment at least, a heritage from imperial Rome.

Bull-fighting was probably well established in the peninsula as early as the eleventh century, but the first Fiesta de Toros recorded was the one which took place at Avila in 1107 on the occasion of the marriage of Blasco Muñoz. There Moors and Christians vied with each other in prowess, and in succeeding ages Fiestas became part of the national festivities. In the early days of bull-fighting the sport was confined to knights and gentlemen. Like the tourney it became the means of testing knightly prowess. There was no fighting on foot, and the horses used were splendid chargers, trained to move quickly and avoid the onslaught of the savage beast. It was in every sense a magnificent sport, testing the skill of both horse and rider.

Peter the Cruel, as his name implies, was a lover of the sport, and carried his ferocity so far that at Burgos, in 1351,

he had the murdered body of Garcilazo
de la Vega thrown from his palace window into the great public square to be
trampled upon by the bulls. But the
great patron of bull-fighting in the middle
ages was King John II., or rather his
clever minister and master, Alvaro de
Luna, the best lance, the most accomplished courtier of Spain. During this
reign a bull-ring was established at Madrid, the shows became more costly, the
flower of the nobility vied with Moorish
cavaliers, and *torear a cavallo* was considered an indispensable accomplishment
of every knight.

Be it said to the credit of Isabella the
Catholic, that she would never witness a
bull-fight, and was only induced to abandon her intention of prohibiting the sport
by a promise on the part of the noble
bull-fighters that the horns of the bull
should be blunted and rendered harmless
by encasing them in leather shields, as
is done in Portugal to-day.

Bull - fighting flourished under the

house of Austria, and the Fiesta given
by Philip IV. on the occasion of the visit
of Charles, Prince of Wales, in 1623, was
one of unusual brilliance. With the
arrival of the Bourbons, however, French
tastes and fashions took possession of
the 'court, and bull-fighting like everything else that was Spanish fell into dis-
favor at court, and was abandoned to
the common people. It was then that
the art of fighting on foot supplanted the
braver sport of *torear a cavallo*.

There were a few Fiestas given by the
Bourbons to appease the popular appe-
tite, but bull-fighting degenerated and
became a rough and tumble scramble or
mere bull-baiting. Then the class of
professional matadors sprang up, first
among whom were Francisco de Romero
and the brothers Juan and Pedro Palomo,
living in the early part of the eighteenth
century. But the master spirit who established the code of tauromachian
honor, practically as it exists to-day, and
reorganized the sport on popular lines,

was José Delgado Candido, known to the populace as Pepe Illo, who died in the plaza at Port St. Mary on the 24th of June, 1771.

It was reserved, however, for that degenerate despot Ferdinand VII. to regenerate the national sport by inducing the dissipated nobles of his court to enter the arena in emulation of the knights of Alvaro de Luna. But Ferdinand did not stop there. The very day that he abolished the University of Seville he granted a royal charter for the establishment of a tauromachian academy in the Andalusian capital. That academy exists to-day, and Seville is the centre of the bull-fighting world. The bull-fighting academy is situated in the suburbs of Seville, near the quarter of the tobacco girls, a wise situation from the standpoint of affiliation. It is supplied with a miniature bull-ring where the students may practice the tauromachian art, and in addition there are stables, sleeping rooms, a restaurant and other appliances for rendering this "University" perfect of its kind.

Bull-fights are expensive luxuries, costing in the neighborhood of $2,000, so that, except on rare occasions, they are given only in Madrid and the provincial capitals. The season commences after Lent and closes in the autumn, Sunday being the day usually chosen for the sport. The profits of the bull fight are often destined for the support of hospitals, and with unintentional irony a fight was once held in Madrid for the benefit of the society for the prevention of cruelty to animals. The larger plazas are under the superintendence of a society of noblemen and gentlemen called maestranzas, established by Philip II. in 1562 for the purpose of improving the breed of Spanish horses. The king is the *hermano mayor*, or elder brother of these tauromachian societies. They are known as the maestranzas of Ronda, Seville, Granada, Valencia and Saragossa, the latter having been established by Ferdinand VII. as the city's reward for its heroic defense against the French. The maestrantes of each city are distinguished by striking uniforms, and as the members must be of gentle blood, the honor of membership is much sought.

The breeding of bulls for the ring is a great industry, and so carefully have the savage traits of the Spanish bull been cultivated that the animal is undoubtedly the most courageous beast in the world. There have been several fights in Madrid in which bulls were pitted against lions, tigers, panthers and even elephants. The bulls were invariably the victors, except in the case of one famous elephant who developed a marvelous adroitness in defending himself with his tusks. The best breed of bulls are those of the Duke of Veragua. His ganadero is situated near Toledo and it is said that when the railway was first built there, the bulls attacked the locomotive without the slightest hesitation. The operation of driving the bulls selected for the ring from the country to the plaza is almost as exciting as the fight itself. The bulls are enticed by tame oxen, "*cabestros*," into a road barricaded on both sides and driven at full speed to the plaza by mounted *conocedores*. The horsemen are armed with long lance-like poles, and the bulls are encouraged by shouts and cries. Crowds are out to welcome the *toros*, and many a beggar who cannot afford the entrance price to the arena, struggles for a front place at the *encierro*, and vents his hostility to the bull by taking a sly poke at one of the doomed animals.

Bull-baiting seems irresistible to the Spaniard of all classes, and even the children play at the national sport in imitation of their elders.

The bull-fight is to Madrid what the Grand Prix is to Paris or the Derby to London. No gayer, sprightlier crowd could be imagined than Spaniards on the way to the plaza de toros; women with their white mantillas and large combs, their fans and their gay garments; men with broad-brimmed hats and short braided jackets; bull fighters in carriages, cheered by the crowd as they pass along; picadors on horseback; soldiers, guardia civiles, street urchins, beggars, mules, donkeys and everything characteristic of the peninsula, are there hurrying merrily towards the arena, all happy, good natured and keenly interested in the national sport.

Inside the amphitheatre the scene is even more spectacular. The crowds of *aficionados*, or " rooters" as they would be called in America, are seating themselves on the stone benches, arguing, betting and discussing the sport in the peculiar vernacular of the bull-ring. Peddlers are selling oranges, shrimps and aguardiente; the band is playing; beautiful women survey the scene from the upper tier of boxes, their black eyes flashing with enthusisam. The effect of color and light, the animation of the scene, are incomparable.

A BULL FIGHT

But the pageant is at its height when
the trumpets blare and the toreadors in
all their glittering gorgeousness march
solemnly across the arena and salute the
president.   There are matadors, chulos,
banderilleros and picadors, the dramatis
personae of the bull ring, headed by
the alguazil or constable, whose sombre
black garments are in funereal contrast
to the bright costumes of the gladiators.
The trumpet sounds again, the president
throws the key of the toril, which the
alguazil catches in his hat, unless he be
unskillful, when he calls forth the hisses
and scoffs of the crowd.   The door of
the den is opened, the bull dashes
amazed and startled into the sandy
arena.

Then the tragedy commences;—a
tragedy calling forth agility, skill, daring, patient suffering, brutal cruelty,
unflinching courage, wild enthusiasm.
But alas, pity is unknown.   The poor
miserable horses, faithful servitors of
man, meet the ferocious onslaught of the

bull with a patience which is heartrending; their bloody entrails cover the sand; they fall and rise again, bearing their brutal riders until the last breath has left them, without calling forth the slightest sign of pity from the Spanish throng. It is "bravo toro, viva toro," or "tunante, cobardo, picaro," according as the bull is brave or poltroon.

When the slaughter of the horses is over and the skillful play of the banderillos commences, one shares the enthusiasm of the sport. The agility with which the darts are placed in the bull's neck is so astonishing that one forgets to pity the bull as he writhes in torture, and like the rest one applauds the matador or killer as he solemnly salutes the president and swears to do his duty.

The duel which follows is actually worthy of the name of sport. It is skill against force; intelligence against passion, and the deliberate play with which the executioner studies the characteristics of his victim before making the final lunge is marvelously fascinating. If the horses could be banished; if the man in the first instance could face the bull alone and vanquish him as he does after the animal's energy is expended and the poor creature only fights with the desperation of the dying, then bull-fighting would be worthy to be classed as sport. But the baiting which precedes the final contest, the torture for the sake of torture, the bloodshed for the sake of bloodshed, is so loathsome that one is disgusted with one's self for succumbing to the excitement and the fascination of the final duel.

Bull-fighting, however, is not the only blood-thirsty sport of the Spaniard, as cocking mains are held every Sunday morning in the Andalusian cities in the Renidero de Gallos or cockpit. The crowds, however, are small and the sport is confined to a few *aficionados* who are mostly annual subscribers. Cock-fighting, however, is a Saxon sport which the Spaniards have transplanted, and as the

Spanish cocks fight without artificial spurs the Spaniards maintain that in this respect at least they are less cruel than the English.

The Renidero is a miniature amphitheatre, covered with a roof. The seats are arranged in tiers, those nearest the ring being reserved for annual subscribers. In the centre there is a low circular platform covered with a coarse matting and surrounded by an iron paling. It is there that the fighting takes place. Suspended from the roof are a pair of crude scales for weighing in the cocks, and in a neighboring room are a number of darkened coops where the birds are kept preparatory to the contest.

The habitués of the cockpit are an interesting lot, sharing the characteristics of the "sporting class" at home; low-browed ruffians, most of them, with brutal faces, and much addicted to loud clothes and brilliant jewelry. One, in particular, would have made a Chicago alderman jealous. He was attired in a

suit of grey plaid with broad black braid.
He wore a frilled shirt ornamented with
an enormous diamond, and his jeweled
watch chain was large enough for a ship's
cable; his trousers were skin tight, with
a broad black stripe along the seam,
and his grey felt hat with enormous brim
was ornamented with a wide black band.
He was fat, and his greasy jowls fell in
folds over his rakish collar; a cigar was
cocked between his lips, and as a typical
"sport" it would be hard to find his
equal. Upon inquiring his calling one
learned that he was a contractor for the
meat of bulls killed in the arena. There
were several bull fighters, too, among
the crowd at the time of one's visit, and
it is doubtful if an American prize fight
could collect a more representative gathering of the sporting fraternity.

The first proceeding in the order of
ceremonies was the weighing in of the
cocks, a function performed with punctil-
ious solemnity. Then the cocks, a white
youngster full of dash, but lacking in

experience, and an old red veteran, who had already lost part of his comb and an eye in previous duels, were placed in the pit. A few preliminary flutters and a dash or two at each other's heads aroused the excitement of the *aficionados*, who stood up in their seats and made bets freely, the veteran cock being the favorite.

At every onslaught of the cocks new bets were made and the enthusiasts grew more excited. The scene resembled the Chicago wheat pit, everyone shouting at once, each trying to find takers for bets without missing a single incident of the contest. Meanwhile the cocks attacked with renewed vigor; feathers flew, blood flowed freely. The tactics adopted by the veteran bird were worthy of a higher intelligence. He let the youngster make the fighting and dodged his onslaughts, then when the fury was spent he attacked his retreating foe vigorously, administering deadly pecks about the head and neck. Finally the younger bird fell exhausted; the scarred veteran uttered an exultant cackle and jumping upon his prostrate foe proceeded to peck out the remaining spark of his life.

After a knock-out a bird is allowed two minutes in which to rise. If he fails to do so within the alloted time, or if at any time the bird refuses to fight and runs away, his rival wins the main. Sometimes the birds are killed outright; sometimes they are temporarily injured.

In an adjoining room is the hospital where the birds are doctored after the fight. Their heads are bathed in arnica and a long feather is shoved down the throat to remove the clotted blood, then the invalid is placed in a darkened coop to recover as best he may.

Cock-fighting is a brutal sport without the pageantry and the deeds of daring which make one forget at moments the brutality of the bull fight.

There is one Spanish sport, however, which is manly and vigorous, a sport comparable to the best of Anglo-Saxon

games.   Pelota de Cesta, or basket ball,
though unlike its Saxon namesake, is
the game of the Basque provinces, but is
now played in the principal cities of
Spain, where elaborate buildings have
been erected for the accommodation of
the players and spectators.

Pelota is a game which in some respect
resembles racquets.   It is played in a
three-sided court about four times the
length of a racquet court; the ball used
is similar to a racquet ball, but instead of
a bat the player has a basket-work scoop
which fits tightly on his hand and fore-
arm.   The game is played with two,
or sometimes more, on a side.   The
court is oblong and enclosed on three
sides.   Along the open space seats and
boxes for the spectators are arranged.
The players station themselves in pairs
consisting of opponents.   The lighter
men are about half way up the court and
the stronger near the end.   The ball is
played the long way of the court.   When
play commences one of the first pair of

players serves the ball against the opposite wall, the other side endeavors to
return it, and the ball remains in play
until a miss is scored for one of the con-
tending sides.   Should the side serving
fail to return the ball the service passes
to the opponents.   A miss scores one for
the opponents and the game usually consists of fifty points.

This, in brief, is an outline of the
game.   There are the usual number of
rules about false strokes, fouls, off-side
play, etc., which accompany games of
the sort, but the fundamental principle
of pelota consists in receiving the ball in
the scoop and whacking it against the
opposite wall.   In that it is very simple,
but the Spanish players display a marvelous amount of agility, and one does
not remember to have seen tennis or
racquets more skillfully played than pelota as done by the best Spanish players.
It is a game which calls for great agility
and extreme endurance.   Play is so rapid
that from the spectator's point of view

it is an extremely interesting performance.

There are occasional periods of rest during which the players seat themselves to catch their breath. They wear a sort of sandal on their feet which they often change several times during the game. The Spaniards are great gamblers, and bets are freely exchanged at pelota matches. Book-makers walk along in front of the spectators offering and taking wagers, and at interesting periods of the game there is much excitement.

Unfortunately pelota is played by professionals, although there are some amateur contests. The games which calls forth crowds are those where the contestants are paid for their services. As the game is of northern origin the best players are from Navarre and the Basque provinces, and the "boina," a cap somewhat resembling a tam-o-shanter, but made of soft felt and without the tuft, the typical head dress of the Carlist armies, is invariably worn by the pelota players.

Pelota is the only manly game the Spaniards have. It certainly compares favorably with the most athletic of our own sports, but like base ball it is robbed of its charm by professionalism and betting. However, after witnessing a pelota match one feels it is a game the Spaniards may well be proud of. It is a genuine sport, and one's hope is that its growth may eventually redeem the country from the curse of bull-fights and cocking mains. A nation's sports are largely typical of its character, and a people capable of tolerating bull fighting is incapable of civilization in its highest sense.

Cordova the Magnificent

CORDOVA the Magnificent, the seat of Arab learning, the birthplace of Seneca, Lucan and Averroes, the splendid capital of the Omeyan Khalifate, with her six hundred mosques and thousand baths, her eight hundred public schools and library of over half a million volumes; Cordova the single shrine where the light of learning glowed during the dark Middle Ages, is to-day a sluggish sun-baked remnant of all that has gone before. Christian bells clang in the Muezzin tower of Islam's fairest mosque, Christian priests mumble their prayers where the Moslem once turned his face to Mecca; but the city is a city of the dead, and the inhabitants are ghouls, if ghouls can be sluggish and ambitionless, for the little vitality they have is drawn from the souls of the departed.

The city is, to be sure, the capital of a province, and one of the eight military centers of the kingdom. There are, to be sure, some fifty thousand inhabitants, most of them dark skinned, ragged loiterers, born only for the artist's brush, but in Cordova, more perhaps than anywhere else in Spain, one is impressed with the ruin which has almost overcome the land.

Toledo was the capital of the Goth, but there is little to mourn for in the Goth. Granada, so often associated with Moorish Spain, was merely the last splendid effort of a decaying race; but Cordova, in its prime, was the vigorous epitome of all that was strong and good in Islam. When Cordova fell Islam fell, for no other city of the Mohammedan world has even attained the intellectual standard set by this capital of the Omeyan Khalifs.

The mosque of Cordova, one begrudges

the name cathedral, is one of the marvels of the world; the city, one of its
mockeries. One might dismiss the city
with a word were it not that in spite of
its dirt and slothfulness it is, in a certain sense, fascinating. One enjoys wandering through the narrow tortuous
streets, with their low whitewashed
houses and dingy little shops, where the
cobbler or the coppersmith are at work
—shops that are a relic of Moorish days,
for they are but the booths of an Oriental bazaar, Christianized by an occasional
picture of a saint or the Virgin. There
is a delight, too, in flattening one's self
against a wall to let a string of meek-
faced donkeys amble by, even if one
falls a prey to the nearest beggar, who,
taking you thus at a disadvantage,
thrusts some festered wound or handless
arm under your very nose.

The beggars of Spain! They deserve
a passing tribute, not to their filth, or
their persistency, but to their courtliness, for each one, if he were washed

and dressed in silks and satins, and given a wand of office, might fill the post of royal chamberlain.

There is a charm, however, to the streets of Cordova in spite of the beggars, which almost makes you forget the glories of the Khalifate. The older portion of the town presents that strange blending of the Oriental and the Occidental which is so typical of the cities of southern Spain. There are the narrow ill-paved streets, the low flat-roofed houses with their hanging balconies and ·white-washed walls you see to-day in Morocco, but instead of mosque and minaret, there is the cold, stern façade of the parish church; instead of the white burnoose of the Arab the black robe of the priest. There is scarcely a straight street in Cordova, and very few wide enough for two carriages to pass. The plan of the city is like one of those mazes where you wander about for hours unable to find your way out, and always returning to the starting point. In roaming through the old town you stumble upon many relics of Roman or Moor, many a graceful archway with its iron grill where a glimpse is caught of some cool shady patio with palms and oranges, and a fountain splashing lazily in its alabaster basin. Here and there in the maze of streets are the imposing façades of patrician houses with carved escutcheons and sombre warriors of stone, standing guard in pillared niches. The most impressive of these portals is that of the Casa de los Paez, now a polythenic school and a station of the electric lighting company. It is the irony of fate to find a network of wires spanning the court of this relic of an ancient family.

Perhaps by chance you may extricate yourself from the network of crooked streets and enter the Calle del Gran Capitan, a broad, dusty boulevard lined with theatres and modern buildings. It is straight and new, and like all things new in Spain, it is ugly; but the Cordovan points with pride to this street and

CASA DE LOS PAEZ

the Paseo beyond as an evidence that his city is progressive. It is progressive, if a few straight streets lined with stuccoed houses and ateliers painted purple and pink constitute progress. There is a park, too, laid out with oppressive regularity, where the municipal band plays on Sundays with fifteen minute intervals between the pieces for the musicians to loiter about and smoke. Soldiers and housemaids gather there, and perhaps a carriage or two of the nobility, with an attempt at style in the form of tarnished gold lace and well-worn liveries; but you turn in disgust from this modern Cordova, and hailing a cab drive away from all those signs of progress back to the old town, where the streets are paved with cobbles and the white Moorish houses are outlined against the blue sky. In your heart you wish that Spain might sleep on forever, the awakening is so harsh and material, so ill-suited to a land of memories.

The streets are so narrow that the

cabman takes a circuitous route around the walls, past gates of tapia and castellated turrets, square or octagon, where the Moorish sentry once paced his weary beat. The Moor is gone, but there are barrack yards, where Christian recruits, undersized and awkward, are drilling for the battle-fields of Cuba. It is pitiful to watch them, they are so ignorant, so docile, mere boys, whipped into shape by their brutish officers, and then packed off to Cuba like so many sheep.

There is a chapel in the suburbs erected to a virgin of supposed healing powers. It is a place typical of Spanish superstition. Locks of hair, crutches, bandages, babies' clothes and every conceivable emblem of the cures effected by the miraculous virgin, have been hung upon the outer walls by grateful convalescents. There are scores of crude paintings, too, representing the Virgin appearing to bedridden sufferers and bidding them rise and walk. Such

places make one understand more readily the power of the priestcraft and the
seemingly hopeless superstition of the
common people. But the Virgin of the
Holy Fountain is charmingly domiciled.
There is a garden surrounding her
chapel with oranges and roses in abundance, and the old crone in attendance
gives one a bouquet and readily accepts
a *propina* in spite of the fact that one
is a heretic. Passing out of the gate
one notices a crude painting of a soul in
purgatory, and fancies the grateful
crone buying masses for the salvation
of her relatives.   To what better use
could the coppers of unbelievers be put?

A few minutes drive, however, leaves
the miraculous virgin and her chapel
far behind, and you are back in the old
town again, where wheeling is difficult
and walking is preferable.   In fact,
walking is preferable nearly everywhere
in Spain, for there are so many odd
nooks to be explored, so many old shops
to peep into, that a cab is a nuisance.

The Land of the Castanet

Instinctively one wanders towards
the river and over the old Roman
bridge to the opposite bank, where the
best view of Cordova is to be obtained.
This bridge over the Guadalquivir is
said by the Arab writers to have been
originally erected by Octavius Cæser,
but it was rebuilt by the Khalifs of
Cordova. Its sixteen arches are crum-
bled and moss-grown now, and instead
of the tramp of Roman legions or the
clatter of Arab horses, there is the delicate tread of patient donkeys wending
their way to the market stall. The
Calahorra tower of the Moors, with its
polygonal barbican and buttresses stands
guard, as it did when St. Ferdinand be-
sieged the town, and when, later, the
knights of Peter the Cruel were halted
by that river bank; but all that is past
and Cordova is sleeping now, lulled by
the rush of the river as it flows swiftly
by the line of the Arab mills stretching
from shore to shore. The white town
beyond rises sharp against the blue sky,

with its prison and its bishop's palace, the domes of its many churches and the mighty cathedral choir towering huge and ugly above the graceful walls of the Moorish mosque, a lasting monument to the shame of Christian vandals. The plain of Cordova stretches flat and barren towards the mountains of Granada, with here and there the crumbling brown walls of a Moorish watch-tower, and beyond the town to the west are the line of blue hills where the absentee nobility have their gardens and their villas.

There is little more of the town that is worth seeing, unless it be the Alcazar, or Khalif's palace. Its remains are now a prison, where some three hundred poor wretches loll in idleness about the foul courts, while the sentry stands guard on the moss-grown towers. The gardens beyond, where the Moorish kings wandered with their harem favorites, are rank with weeds; a few basins of sluggish water remain to mark the

Moorish baths, but the Alcazar is little more than a memory.

The one sight of Cordova, however, the one point of surpassing interest, is the great mosque of Abdur-Rahmin I., the Zecca of the west, with its mihrab, or holy of holies, equivalent in the eyes of the ancient Moslem pilgrim to the caaba of the prophet at Mecca. This mosque is the most perfect example of Moorish religious architecture in existence or ever erected. It was built in the most powerful period of Mohammedan rule, and it is typical of its builders; for its style, unlike the Alhambra, is simple but vigorous, its proportions grand. There is none of the effeminate minuteness and delicate, almost lace-like stucco work, so redolent of dark-eyed beauties and soft perfumes found in the later Grenadine work. On the contrary the mosque of Cordova is severe, massive and vast, with simple curves, and impressive vistas. One is bewildered by the seemingly interminable forest of pillars spanned by countless arches. What the interior must have been when the roof was glistening with vivid colors, and thousands of gold and silver lamps, when its arches were studded with emeralds and rubies, is beyond conception. Now the rude whitewash brush of the Christian vandal has marred the delicate walls and a Christian choir, magnificent to be sure, but destroying the simplicity of the plan, has been reared in the center of the edifice, where Christian priests may chant the glories of the conqueror. One spot only, the mihrab or sanctuary of the Moslem, gives one a partial impression of the former glories of this mosque. The walls of this mihrab form a heptagon, the pavement is of marble, and the shell-shaped roof, also of marble, is hewn from a single block; the walls are decorated with three lobed arches resting on marble pillarets, and the mosaic ornamentation of the cupola, the work of Greek artists from Constantinople, surpasses the finest examples of

Byzantine art in Italy or the east. The flint glass and metals of this work actually have the appearance of velvet and gold brocade. In the mihrab the unparalleled pulpit of Al Haken II. was kept. It was of ivory and precious wood and stones, fastened with gold and silver nails. It contained the Koran made by Othman and stained with his blood. A box covered with gold tissue and embroidered with pearls enclosed this precious relic. But the feet of Moslem pilgrims no longer tread the pavement of this shrine; Christian incense burns before the high altar and the chant of priests echoes from the choir.

When St. Ferdinand the Conqueror entered the captured city of Cordova his first act was to purify the mosque and dedicate it to the Virgin. Several chapels and altars were added, but it was not until later, in 1521, that the great trançept and choir were begun. This latter work was designed by Hernan Ruiz and finished by his son Diego de

THE CHOIR, CORDOVA CATHEDRAL

Praves. It is in style morisco, gothic and plateresque. The high chapel and the choir form a cathedral in themselves, but the huge retablo of bronze and jasper, and the sixty-three choir-stalls, minutely carved from mahogany, by Pedro Cornejo, though unexcelled, are all out of place. This work is merely a conventional cathedral reared in the centre of the grandest of Moslem edifices by prelates who felt that in christianizing the great mosque they were glorifying God. It was an act of sixteenth century bigotry, but even in those days there were protests against this desecration. The municipal corporation, with a judgment rare in such bodies, cried out against the prelates whose bigotry led to such a profanation, but the emperor, Charles V., unacquainted with the nature of the work contemplated, gave his acquiescence, so the centre of that noble forest of pillars was hewn away to give place for Hernan Ruiz' monument of intolerance. Charles

lived to regret the sacrilege he had
permitted, for, on passing through Cordova a few years later, he reproved the
chapter by exclaiming: "You have
built here what you or anyone might
have built anywhere else; but you have
destroyed what was unique in the world."

An open court is the essential feature
of Andalusian architecture, and even the
mosque is not without its patio. Said
Ben Ayub added the Patio de Los Naran-
jos (Court of the orange trees) to the
mosque of Cordova in 937, and its rows
of trees originally corresponded with the
lines of columns in the mosque. One
likes to tarry there under the shade of
the Moorish walls and watch the groups
of idlers loitering about the moss-grown
fountain, the scene is so semi-Moor-
ish, so characteristic of southern Spain.
Dark-haired girls wrapped in the bright-
colored shawls so dear to the Andalusian lean upon their earthen water jars
and gossip; bright-eyed urchins play in
the listless way of Spain, and beggars

loll in the sun while the water trickles into the old stone basin and the wind soughs through the leaves of palms and orange trees. It is a place to while the hours away and dream of the departed glories of Cordova the great, the most luxurious, the most civilized city of mediæval Europe.

An Arab poet has written on Cordova the following distich: "Do not talk of the court of Baghdad and its glittering magnificence; do not praise Persia and China and their manifold advantages; for there is no spot on earth like Cordova, nor in the whole world men like the Beni Hamdin."

One believes in the truthfulness of this poet when one reads what the old Moorish authorities say of Cordova in the days of its glory. The city at one time covered a space of ground ten miles in length, all lighted at night by lamps; the walls around the Alcazar of the Khalif were two leagues and three quarters long; the city was divided into five large districts separated from one another by high and well fortified walls, while the suburbs are said to have been twenty-one in number, each provided with mosques, markets and baths. The traveler, before arriving, had some foretaste of the luxury awaiting him, for manzils, or rest houses, were provided on the principal highways for the gratuitous entertainment of travelers. The gates of Cordova were seven in number, and in the midst of the city stood the Kassabah, or citadel. But all the edifices were not of a warlike nature, for the Khalif had his palace of contentment, his palace of flowers, his palace of lovers, and fairest of all, his palace of Damascus; while the humble Moslem spent his leisure hours in the Golden Meadow, the Garden of the Waterwheel, or the Meadow of Murmuring Waters. Without the city was a palace built over the Guadalquivir on arches, and a palace called Dimashk, of which a poet said:

"All palaces in the world are nothing

when compared to that of Dimashk, for not only has it gardens filled with the most delicious fruits and sweet-smelling flowers, beautiful prospects and limpid running waters, clouds fragrant with aromatic dew, and lofty buildings,

"But its earth is always perfumed, for morning pours on it her grey amber and night her black musk."

Oriental extravagance, to be sure, but extravagant only in metaphor.

More marvelous even than Cordova was the suburb and palace of Az Zahra. One third of the revenues of the state were devoted to the building of this royal whim by Abdur Rahman the Great, for a period of twenty-five years, and for fifteen years more the work was continued by his son. But not a vestige of this marvelous creation remains, not one stone upon another to mark the site of a fairy edifice, of which it is said no words could paint the magnificence. The enclosing wall was four thousand feet in length, from east to west, and two thousand two hundred from north to south. Four thousand three hundred columns of rarest marble from Africa, Rome and Constantinople, supported the roof of this palace; the halls were paved with marble laid in a thousand various patterns; the cedar ceilings were ornamented with gilding on azure ground, with damask work and interlacing designs; while the surrounding gardens were filled with marble fountains and kiosks, where the sultanas passed their idle hours.

The greatest triumph of Cordova, however, was not in its palaces and mosques, but in its learning and liberality. When Christian Europe was imbrued in barbarian ignorance and superstition, the arts, philosophy and literature, medicine, surgery and chemistry flourished at the capital of the Omeyan Khalif; when the Christian world was steeped in bigotry, Christian worship was tolerated and even encouraged by the Moorish rulers. Christian Spain has never attained the preëminence in learning and liberality of Moorish Cordova. The Khalifs encouraged writers and men of science, and the researches of Hisham, the munificence of Abdur Rahman, the well-endowed universities of Moorish Spain, made Cordova the resort of students and philosophers: thus learning thrived even in the blackest moments of Italian ignorance and papal oppression.

Within fifty years after Hildebrand triumphed at Canossa, Abn'l Walid Mohammed Ibn Ahnad Ibn Mohammed Ibn Rosht was born at Cordova. This man, known to the European world as Averroes, the preserver of Aristotle, was but one among many learned doctors in the schools of Cordova. He enjoyed but little reputation among his compeers save as a clever physician, for he founded no school in Islam, and his fame is due to Christian doctors, who discussed and misunderstood his commentaries, rather than to his fellow countrymen. The works of Averroes had the misfortune or good luck to incur the deadly hatred of the followers of the Spanish Dominic, and thus this Arab student stands before the world as the greatest doctor and most learned philosopher of Moorish Spain; a prophet not without honor save in his own country, while the names of Abubacer, Abenzoor and the scores of other philosophers, scientists and poets who made the name of Cordova great, have been forgotten. Even the fame of Avenpace would have perished had not the great Averroes criticised his philosophy.

In those days of Cordova's glory, when the bigotry of the Spaniard was rife, as it has been in all ages, the Spanish priests, tolerated, even encouraged by the Khalifs, despised the culture of Cordova, and alone among the subject population hated the Moors with bitter and undying hatred. Unwilling to accept even toleration, they publicly reviled the prophet, and courted death

rather live under the liberal government
of the Khalifs. Perfectus and Eulogius
and the other so-called martyrs of Cordova were intolerant fanatics, who cried
aloud in the great mosque of Cordova
that the "Kingdom of Heaven is reserved for the Christians; for the Moslem
miscreants is prepared the fires of Hell."
That spirit is not dead in Spain. It
is too lasting, too time-honored to die,
and to-day the natural heirs of Eulogius
dwell in the hills near Cordova, and turn
their bigoted eyes on the fair plain below.
There is a hermitage in those hills of
ascetic monks where the tonsured, barefooted brothers, some fifteen in number,
follow the austere rules of Peter the
hermit. The view from their retreat is
one to be remembered. Below is the
flat, treeless plain of Cordova, with the
silvery river and the white city gleaming
in the sunlight, and beyond, the snow-
capped mountains of the Sierra Nevada
are outlined against the blue sky. There,
stretched beneath an olive tree, one

gazes at the charming panorama, and wonders at the mutability of all worldly things. Cordova the great is merely a memory; but there are those droning friars, the relics of that intolerance and bigotry which have been the curse of Spain. The Moorish civilization is gone, and the Spanish power which succeeded has waned; but the voice of the chanting monk is still raised as in the days of Eulogius. However, it is fainter now, and the world heeds it less. Perhaps it will soon be hushed forever, and with its silence a new era will begin for Spain— an era of liberty, prosperity and enlightenment.

Granada the Fallen

THERE are views one can never forget, scenes which have an imperishable memory. There can be, however, no impression more lasting than one's recollection of the view from the Vela tower of the Alhambra. Below are the red battlements of the Moorish fortress, and across the rushing Darro the grey-white town is piled high on the hill tops. Beyond the jumble of tile roofs and hanging balconies, the green Vega of Granada, dotted with olives and poplars and the glinting walls of villages, stretches like a carpet of plush towards the purple mountains of Malaga. To the north the rugged Sierra Nevada raise their snow-capped peaks above the clouds, and high on the hillside beyond the towers of the Alhambra, the white arcades of the Generalife glisten in the sunlight.   Myrtles and oranges grow amid the crumbling ruins at one's feet; across the river a Carthusian monastery, perched like a sentinel of Christ upon a hilltop, proudly overlooks the troublous Albeicin quarter and recalls stern Ximines and his unrelenting treatment of the conquered Moor.   But wherever one turns there are memories.   There is a gate where the hapless Boabdil's lance was shattered as he went forth to disaster, and across the Vega the grey towers of the Santa Fé, reared by the invading host of the Catholic kings, rise dimly from the plain.   In fancy one sees the smoke of the conqueror's torch or the dust of Moorish cavalry.

But those days are over; Granada the beautiful sleeps.   There in the town below mice-like donkeys tread their patient way beside the rumbling Darro, while ghost-like Spaniards in flowing cloaks silently come and go.   Bells toll, the mournful cries of street venders

mingle with the ripple of waters, the air has the soft stillness of summer, and the lazy beggars dozing in the sun make one know that the Granada of long ago is only a glorious dream.

To speak of Granada is to speak of the Alhambra, but one falters at describing the vastness and the delicacy of that last effort of the Spanish Moor; one falters at treading in Irving's footsteps even in the humblest way, for he made the place and all its memories so thoroughly his own. The hotel beneath the walls bears his name; his "Tales" are sold by importunate venders; the guide shows the rooms in which he slept with an air of mysterious reverence, and wherever one turns one feels the presence of the American writer who, more than any man, has preserved the memory of the Moor. But all the world does not read Irving to-day; his style lacks the crispness and smartness of the up-to-date novelist, and there may be some to whom the "Conquest of Granada" and "Tales of the Alhambra'' are merely the names of unread books.   That is one's only excuse for writing of Granada.

The Alhambra has been called a palace-fortress, and such it certainly was in the days of its prime.   It was almost a city as well, and so numerous were the buildings clustered upon the long promontory, or ridge, raising between the rivers Darro and Genil, that the place was called by the Arabs, Medinah Alhamra, or Alhambra City.   The name has been usually considered to mean ''red castle,'' from the reddish color of the ferruginous tapia work of the walls. It is, however, more probably derived from Kasru-l-hamra, meaning the sultan's palace (Kasr being a corruption of Cæsar), but whatever be the origin of the name, the Alhambra of to-day is of far more recent workmanship than most of the Moorish ruins of Spain.   Although the promontory where the palace stands was long fortified as a stronghold, the Alhambra is practically the creation

of Ibn l Ahmar, the founder of the Mas-
rite dynasty, and dates from about 1248
A. D.

The kingdom of Granada was the last
stronghold of the Moors in the Peninsula;
Cordova was the capital of Moorish
Spain in its prime, and on the breaking
up of the Omeyan Khalifate after the
death of Almanzor in 1002, into numerous petty kingdoms, Seville rose to the
greatest prominence. The feuds between these petty kingdoms were nearly
successful in destroying the Arab power
entirely. And had not the Almoravides
and the Almohades, two fanatical sects
from Africa, invaded Spain successively
in the interests of the Crescent, the end
of Moslem rule might have been ante-
dated some four centuries. But the
semi-barbarous tribes from Africa infused
new vigor into the declining Moor and
prolonged the Mohammedan power. It
was not until the great Christian victory
of Navas de Tolosa, in 1212, that the
power of the Almohades was crushed.

The Land of the Castanet

The fall of Cordova and Seville was but a question of a few years. Granada, one of the petty Arab kingdoms, became the last refuge of the Moor. The Moslem, driven from Cordova, Seville and the other cities of Spain, sought shelter in this little mountain kingdom, and there for two centuries the decadent Moors, by wisely acknowleding the suzerainty of the kings of Castile, were enabled to govern themselves and prolong their final downfall.

The Grenadine, like all decadents, was luxurious, effeminate and contentious. His history is a history of palace intrigues, rebellions and civil wars; when he was not fighting the Christian he was plotting, and his idle moments were spent with the women of his harem, surrounded by all the luxury his ingenuity could devise. His art was delicate and refined, but it lacked the vigor shown in the works of the Cordovans. Its very effeminacy, however, gives it a charm which has made the Alhambra rank first in interest among the Moorish ruins. One pities a fallen race, one has sympathy for a people who, like the Grenadines, were the remnant of a mighty power. That is, perhaps, why the two centuries of Granada's history have almost over-shadowed the five centuries of Moorish grandeur at Cordova. The last struggle of the Moors against the power of the Catholic kings has been the topic of many a romance and poem, and Boabdil the miserable rebel, the tool of women, the traitor, has become a hero at the expense of his brave father and still braver uncle, merely because it was he who surrendered the keys of Granada to Ferdinand and Isabella, and because as he looked for the last time upon the towers of the Alhambra, he stood "crying like a woman for the kingdom he could not defend like a man." What a pitiful successor to the great Abdur Rahman Almanzor, or even Al Ahmar, the founder of Boabdil's house! Yet the average reader, if he knows of the Moors at all, knows of Boabdil. The great names of Moorish history have been forgotten that the name of the rebel and traitor may live. Likewise the Alhambra has attained a preëminence perhaps undeserved in point of grandeur, but certainly not in point of beauty; for this fairy palace of the declining Moor stands unique among the world's monuments.

The earlier phase of Moorish art, exemplified by the mosque of Cordova, was the outcome of a stern, almost ascetic spirit, which avoided frivolous ornamentation, and reflected the vigorous character of the times. The Alhambra belongs to the last period of Moorish architecture, a degenerate period wanting in lofty inspiration, and expressing the effeminacy and luxury of the age. It is almost excessive in ornamentation, the proportions are even paltry, and there is exaggeration in the outline; but no other Moorish monument possesses the delicate refinement, the almost inex-

COURT OF THE MYRTLES (ALHAMBRA)

pressible charm of this palace of the
Grenadine kings.

How many times has the Alhambra
been described minutely? As often as a
traveler with a pencil and a note book
has wandered within its walls. It has
been called a fortress, a castle, a palace,
a city, a ruin, a monument, and one
knows not what else; each stone, each
azulejo, has received its share of attention, and the end is not yet. One prefers to saunter quietly through the shady
courts, tarrying for a moment here and
there, and leaving minute description to
the architect or the antiquary.

In the Plaza de los Algibes (Place of
the Cisterns) for instance, you may rest
for a while in the shade of a crumbling
wall and study the history of Spain ob-
jectively. Surrounding you are the
irregular walls and square castellated
towers of the fortress, the entrance to
the Moorish palace, the church of San
Nicolas, the unfinished Tuscan palace

of Charles V., and the houses of the
Alhambra leeches, who thrive on travelers. One sees at a glance the vestiges
of Roman rule and Arab dominion, side
by side with the monumental evidence of
Spanish fanaticism and Austrian conceit;
while lolling in the sun are the slothful
Spaniards of to-day, typical of a greatness which has waned.

But it is impossible to tarry unmolested in the Plaza de los Algibes. Just
when one's fancy is turning to the romantic period of Moorish rule and pic-
turing that palace yard filled with
bearded Moors, resplendent with colored
silks and jeweled cimeters, white turbans
and glistening lances, the self-styled
"Prince of The Gypsies" thrusts his
smirking countenance before one's face
and begs for a copper to keep his royal
highness in aguardiente. This picturesque ruffian was once a model for Fortuny, and he now attires himself in
fantastic garb and preys upon the unwary tourist. He is but one of a host

of miscreants haunting the Alhambra, and dogging one's footsteps. To escape one must enter the palace itself, where the employés are civil and one is left unmolested to enjoy the delights of Moorish art.

Of all the courts of the Alhambra that of the Lions is most universally known. It is a perfect model of the Moorish patio, and the light, graceful columns, the open filagree work, the colored tiles, the stalactite arches, are so admirably blended that criticism seems futile. The fountain, too, with its huge alabaster basin, supported by twelve heraldic lions, is a familiar friend one has known in story and picture from childhood. There is a view across this court which for its delicacy and charm is unrivalled. You must make friends with the empleado who paces to and fro on the marble pavement, eyeing the visitors who come and go. It is his duty to protect the court from defacement, and the relic-hunting tourist is his enemy; but with a word or two of greeting, and the offer of a cigarillo, he becomes your friend, and with rare attention he fishes out an old chair from behind some column and places it for you in the cool shady entrance to the Hall of the Abencerrages. Not only does he thus provide for your comfort, but he discreetly retires to a neighboring hall and leaves you to unmolested enjoyment of the place.

One looks across the court, where griffin-like lions gaze heavenward, to the Hall of the Two Sisters. Broad marble steps descend gently, lace-like arches are grouped in bewildering perspective, some white, some delicate flesh color, with here and there pale tints of pink and blue. Behind the fountain a network of stalactite archways, deep in shadow, converge to the double mirador of the " Favorite," where alabaster columns glisten in the sunlight, and orange and cypress trees spread their brilliant green branches in the Lindaraja garden beyond.

Granada the Fallen

In the hall where one is sitting, the dark ferruginous blotches on the pavement are said to be the blood stains of the Abencerrages, a powerful family of Granada, murdered by the miserable Boabdil as the tyrant's reward for their assistance in placing him upon his father's throne. It is one of the legends of the Alhambra, more reliable than the stains upon the floor. But one dislikes to examine the fables of the Moor under the cold light of history. One prefers rather the romantic tales of Irving; tales of fair sultanas and their Christian captive lovers, of cruel khalifs and plotting viziers. One listens in fancy to the rattle of the cimeter and the tramp of bearded warriors, and pictures in imagination the dark eyes of harem favorites glancing from the miradores above upon lithe dancing girls moving to the sonorous lute and the clash of cymbals in the court below; while luxurious Moors, reclining on silken divans, sip fragrant sherbet from golden cups, and

Nubian slaves slowly fan the summer
air.

The Alhambra is bewilderment. Everywhere one turns there is grace in outline and charm in color. One wanders
through halls and galleries with maze-like
arches and myriad columns, where Ara-
bic legends are intricately interwoven
in countless designs. There are shady
courts where goldfish play in marble
basins, and the shadows of myrtle
hedges are cast upon the green water;
there are delicate balconies set in the
outer walls, where one gazes from dizzy
heights upon the rushing Darro and the
white town sprinkled on the hillside;
there are crumbling towers with fairy
chambers, where sultanas dwelt, and
mosques and baths, and halls of justice.
One confesses an inability even to enu-
merate the delights of the Alhambra, for
there is fascination everywhere.

Those Grenadine kings, however,
were not content with their palace fortress. In the hot summer months they

GENERALIFFE, GRANADA

retired to the hillside above, where the white villa of the Generalife looks down upon the Alhambra. The name General-ife is said to signify "Garden of the Dance." The Grenadine kings took care that the place should not belie its name. It was used for festival occasions and to pass the idle moments; a villa of revelry and pleasure, where the sensuous Moor might indulge in his favorite pleas-ures. Neglect and the whitewash brush have marred the delicate stucco work, but the many fountains and the gardens with their orange and lemon trees, their evergreen arches and yews twisted into fantastic patterns, give partial evi-dence of the charms of the Generalife in the days of its prime. One understands the flowery praise of Arab poets. It is a pleasure to tarry in those gardens. The fountains murmur, and the leaves or oranges are vivid in the sunlight. The tall forms of cypresses cast cool shadows on the pavement, and the odor of roses scents the air. One's thoughts turn to long ago, and in fancy the hosts of the Catholic kings are marshalled in the plain below; pennons flutter, the armor of Christian knights glistens as their restless chargers paw the ground. Ferdinand and Isabella are there, and Gonzalo de Cordova, "the great captain," whose fame is soon to resound through Europe; stern Mendoza, too, and all the Christian soldiers and prelates, who for ten long years have been waging relentless war upon the Moor. It is the hour of triumph for the cross, for hapless Boabdil comes forth from the city gates to surrender the keys of Granada to the conqueror. The story of the Moor is ended, and the banner of Castile, hoisted by the hand of Cardinal Mendoza, flutters from the Vela tower. Spain becomes a Christian nation.

It was a marvelous period in her history, for Columbus went forth that year from Palos. He was present in the besieging camp of Santa Fé pleading his cause. Weary and disgusted by temporizing, he turned his face toward France, and was on his way across the Vega, when a messenger from the queen overtook him, and he came back to add another world to Castile-Leon.

Spain was given a glorious chance, but the Spanish Christian, like the Moor, was unequal to the task. Four hundred years have passed, and the world looks on to-day at Spain's desperate struggle to retain the last possessions of her mighty empire. "There is no conqueror but God." That is the sentiment chiselled in a hundred places on the walls of the Alhambra. It was the sentiment of the fatalistic Moor, but the lazy Spaniard who lolls there in the sun to-day, if he thinks at all, should realize its truth, as exemplified over and over again in the history of his country.

The Granada of to-day is a sluggish Spanish city, with narrow winding streets where idlers congregate. The houses are taller than those of Seville, with more balconies, but the walls are not so white, and there are few of those delightful courts with fountains and flowers which lend a holiday air to the rival city. Granada is more like a Castilian than an Andalusian city, and there is little to attract the visitor who wanders down the steep Alhambra hill into the town below. Curiosity shops are there to entrap the unwary traveler, and in some of the narrower streets there are attractive dashes of local color in the shape of dingy booths, and donkeys, and tattered beggars. There are pretty girls, too, leaning on the balconies, their spirited eyes flashing defiance at cloaked gallants lounging in the sun; but the town has a forlorn air of "decayed gentility."

The women, however, almost redeem the city, for nowhere in Spain are there such marvelous complexions as one sees in Granada. There is a delicate softness to the skin, and a rich flush of color, which combined with the glossy hair and piercing black eyes, form the perfect Spanish type of beauty. The beauty is facial, however, as few Spanish women have good figures, and they waddle rather than walk. In the simple black dresses and lace mantillas which they wear going to mass, they are the Spanish women of one's imagination; but in French bonnets and gowns they are fat and awkward. In Granada, however, one sees them even to better advantage than in Seville.

Some ten or fifteen years ago, at the time of a former visit, national costumes were almost universal in Andalusia—the manola dress, with short skirt and silken shawl wrapped about the shoulders, the high comb and lace mantilla; but now even the dancing girls wear clothes of modern pattern. The men, too, used to wear the bolero jacket and skin-tight breeches, the palainas or leggins, the faja or broad sash, and the calañes , or round hat, with two balls or ponpons, one sees so often in Carmen; but now that costume is only found in the coun-

try far from the larger cities; and of
national garments only the capa or
cloak remains; that, too, is disappearing.
The Spaniard, like the Japanese, when
modernized loses his character. What
a pity he does not realize it.

Granada, like all the cities of Spain,
has its cathedral, a Græco-Roman pile,
built in 1529, on the site of the great
mosque. It was intended by the architect to be second to no church in the
world, except perhaps St. Peter's, but
it is second to many in Spain. The proportions are good, but the building is
crowded among the surrounding houses
so that it is not seen to advantage, and
the interior, though simple, one might almost say grand, has been too thoroughly
renovated to possess the sombre charm
of such edifices as the cathedrals of Seville, Toledo and Burgos. There is
much that is gaudy, too, in the coloring,
and the general effect is disappointing.

One's interest in the cathedral centres
in the royal chapel where Ferdinand and

Isabella are buried. This chapel is
really independent of the cathedral, as it
has its own chapter and chaplains. The
interior has the impressive gloom absent
in the larger church; there are slender
palm-like pillars of unusual charm, and
the bassi relievi of the retablo, representing the surrender of Granada and the
conversion of infidels, recalls the stirring times when the Moor was conquered. Effigies of Ferdinand and Isabella kneel beside the altar, and in
the centre of the chapel are the alabaster sepulchres of the Catholic kings,
with those of Phillip I. and crazy Jane
at either side. On the walls are sculptured the words: '' This chapel was
founded by the most Catholic Don Fer-
nando and Doña Isabel, King and Queen
of Spain, of Naples, of Sicily and Jerusa-
lem, who conquered this kingdom and
brought it back to our faith; who acquired the Canary Isles and Indies, as
well as the cities of Oran, Tripoli and
Bugia, who crushed heresy, expelled the

Moors and Jews from these realms and reformed religion."

One stops to ponder on the lifework of those Catholic kings, a work that should have made of Spain a nation such as England is to-day, and as one ponders, the words "who crushed heresy, expelled the Moors and Jews from these realms and reformed religion," stand out preëminent. There is the secret of the failure of Spain.

Wherever one turns in Granada there are historical lessons. In the church of San Geronimo, one of the many interesting sacred edifices which are scattered through the city, Gonzalo de Cordova lies buried. He was the greatest soldier Spain ever produced, a man who more than any other created the European Empire of the Spaniard, who revolutionized the art of war, who over and over again defeated the best troops of France with greatly inferior numbers, and maintained the Spanish power in Italy without money and without men, only to be rewarded by the base ingratitude of his master, the miserly and crafty Ferdinand. The two men who created the magnificent empire of the Catholic Kings were Columbus and Gonzalo de Cordova, "The Great Captain." Each died of a broken heart. Ingratitude is the reward of kings.

One of the sights of Granada which the tourist invariably sees is the gypsy quarter. It is the stock in trade of the guides, and the dances organized there at exorbitant rates, are usually successful in entrapping the unwary traveler. Among the filthy, miserable, unprincipled vagabonds of Christendom, the Grenadine gypsies hold preëminence. They live in a series of caves, dug in the hillside across the Darro, and their sole means of livelihood is fleecing the strangers. The moment a traveler appears within sight of the gypsy quarter he is surrounded by a clamorous, yelling mob of filthy urchins, who dog his footsteps with appalling persistency. The

dance he is to witness takes place in a
dingy, foul smelling hut, with dirt floor
and smoky walls. You are seated in
state in a rickety chair, and told that the
price agreed upon is not sufficient to
insure the full performance. The guitarist needs a larger share, four girls cannot
do all the dances, for a few dollars more
you can see the entire show. After a
great deal of squabbling and gesticulat-
ing the bargain is finally comsummated.
Then the imposition begins. The dancing girls are fat, ugly creatures in gaudy
cotton gowns, whose vulgarity excels
anything seen in the Midway during the
World's Fair, and as the performance
progresses their movements become more
and more objectionable. The leader
who plays the guitar is a clever performer and executes some really excellent
music between the dances, but the foul
place, the vulgar dancers, the gaping
crowd of beggars in the doorway, all make
one thankful to flee from the gypsy
quarter and its disgusting inhabitants.

Granada the Fallen

Escaping from the gypsies you walk back through the old Moorish section of the city known as the Albeicin quarter. The Arab houses are still there, and you can roam leisurely through the narrow streets peeping into the little shops and the quaint old courts, with their Moorish arches and their fountains, their white-washed walls and cool balconies, where vines are growing and dark-skinned girls are leaning on the railings.

There are many excursions to be made about Granada, drives across the Vega to Santa Fé, drives along the gorge of the Darro to the Colegiata del Sacro Monte, with its subterranean chapels erected to commemorate numberless miracles and treasure trove. If you have the time there are excursions to the Alpuxarra mountains, so historic-ally interesting as being the last home of the Moors, and the scene of that frightful series of wars succeeding the fall of Granada, where Don John of Austria won his spurs, and the remnants of the Moors, known as the Moriscos, defied the power of Spain. The great rebellion of the Alpuxarras lasted for two years, and its records of assassination, treachery, brutality and reckless deeds of daring are among the most horrible and fascinating of history. But wherever one turns there is historical association, interesting and sorrowful.

Some six miles from Granada there is a hamlet called Zubia, deserving a special commendation as being the only place in Spain where one did not meet a beggar. But Zubia has another interest. During the siege of Granada, Isabella rode there from the camp at Santa Fé to obtain a view of the Alhambra and the promised land of the Moor. A sally was made from the city and the queen escaped capture — miraculously, of course.

A shrine to the virgin who appeared visibly for the queen's protection was erected by Isabella to commemorate the escape, and its ruins still remain among

GATE OF JUSTICE (ALHAMBRA)

the laurels and the cypress trees. One tarries there for a last view of white Granada scattered over its four hills, and the red Alhambra outlined against the purple mountains beyond. The snow caps of the Sierra Nevada sparkle in the sunlight, the green Vega stretches towards Malaga and the sea, fleecy clouds hang motionless in the hazy sky. The air is balmy, and loitering there one breathes a last sigh for the Moor, who made of Spain the centre of arts and sciences, the seat of learning and refinement. Spain, during the brief brilliancy of the Catholic kings and the Hapsburg Empire was a mighty nation, but it shone with the borrowed light of the Moor. The Moor was banished, but his best memorial lies in the desolate tracts of land where his vines and olives once grew; in the sleepy, ignorant cities where his art and learning once flourished.

Provincial Towns

IN a provincial town away from the beaten tracks of travel, one sees Spanish life as it has existed untainted for centuries. A hundred years at least behind the world, the town sleeps on, undisturbed by modern unrest. Even the railway with its one crawling train per day, skirts along the suburbs a mile or more away as though fearful to disturb the quiet by its pretence of activity.

About the little stuccoed station a group of vagos loiter in the sun, their bronzed faces animated by idle curiosity, their gay mantas slung carelessly across their tattered coats. There is a buffet, too, with its huge bottles of red and yellow wine, its piles of oranges and sour bread. Perchance the train bears a contingent of recruits for Cuba, and

the poor fellows hurriedly crowd around
the wine puesto, and exhaust the
meagre stock of liquids. They are
apparently happy, singing and laughing
to keep their courage up, but the tearful
faces of the peasant women, and the
stoical old men who are there to take a
last farewell of the poor boys, betray the
suffering that war is causing. The inevitable pair of civil guards, with neat black
uniforms and glistening equipments, are
there to scrutinize the crowd with the
authoritative air of the trained policeman.

Spanish trains do not worry much
about time. When the engine driver has
finished his cigarette and the station
master has sufficiently discussed political
gossip with the guard, someone rings a
bell, a whistle is blown, a bell is rung
again, and finally after much gesticula-
tion and waving of hands, with perhaps a
faint attempt at a cheer on the part of
the recruits, the train draws slowly away
and you are left standing on the platform
admiring the temerity of the men who

invaded such a land with locomotives
and iron rails.

Outside the station two or three crude
omnibuses are waiting. There is a dusty
line of road with a double row of trees,
and beyond is the brown mass of the
town with the inevitable cathedral spires
towering against the sky. Seating yourself in one of the omnibuses amid a
crowd of Spanish provincials, you are
hurried away over the hard road towards
the sleepy town. Bells jangle, hoofs
click, the bus sways like a ship at sea,
but the stoical Spaniards about you
smoke on unmoved.   The air is crisp and
chill, and their faces are half hidden in
their muffled cloaks; they utter a few
guttural sounds about the weather, and
perhaps give their cloaks an extra twist.
Finally the walled town is reached, and
the omnibus is halted by the octroi
officials, who proceed to examine the
remotest corners of the vehicle in their
search for dutiable merchandise.   The
driver of the mixed team of mules and

A PROVINCIAL TOWN

horses is a wag, and makes sarcastic remarks about bread contained in his hat and aguardiente in his stomach which he supposes is dutiable, but unmindful of his wit the customs officers proceed in their search until they are satisfied. Then the bus rattles on over the cobbles of the narrow street, scattering goats and chickens to right and left, crowding donkeys and wayfarers against the walls.

The driver is an artist in his line, and he swings his mules and horses about the corners and grazes the walls in a hair-breadth manner which is fairly startling.

Finally the bus enters a street, straighter and wider than the rest, with arcades and a few shops, with colored calicos hanging in the windows. There is even an advertisement of Singer Sewing Machines placarded on a stucco wall, but before you have had time to recover from astonishment at this incongruous evidence of modernism, the huge vehicle stops before a door, where you read the sign "Fonda de Europa" painted dingily over the door. The smirking fondista is there to greet you, and hungry and shivering you descend in the hope of finding warmth and comfort. But alas, it is colder within doors than outside, where the sun tempers the chilly air. There is a cheerless café downstairs where a few of the "quality" of the town are hidden behind copies of "El Imparcial" and "El Liberal." The pavement is stone, and the wind whistles through every crack and crevice of the squeaky old door and windows. The fumes of a single charcoal brazier asphyxiate the air without adding one degree to the warmth. In self defense you are driven to strong drink, but even the aguardiente which the cigarette smoking waiter brings you fails to warm your shivering body. There is no cold which penetrates like Castilian cold. In the sun when walking it is possible to keep warm, but indoors, no matter

how warmly one may be clothed, it
penetrates to the marrow.

At the breakfast hour you wander into
the cheerless dining room and take your
seat at the long table, bowing in Spanish
fashion to each of the guests. The
assemblage is composed of the Spanish
bourgeoisie, and it would be difficult to
find persons more unattractive. A fat
old man with a forbidding scowl occupies
the head of the table, his skin is oily and
his head is bald; he is talking vocifer-
ously and shoveling in food with his
knife between the words. He is evidently a guest of importance in the commercial sense, for the waiter serves him
obsequiously. Next him is a bride from
Bilboa, with her shop-keeper husband.
Like most young Spanish women, she
has the olive skin blended with dark red,
which is so attractive a feature of Spanish beauty. Her abundant hair has a
rare gloss, and her large black eyes are
soulful, but alas, she eats with her knife
and picks her teeth. She is dull, too,

and has little intelligence beyond animal instincts. Her husband has keen little eyes which twitch excitedly. His napkin covers the greater portion of his bosom, and he seems to live to eat, judging by the way he consumes his gazpacho. There is a drummer from Madrid who shows his metropolitan superiority in his contemptuous manner, and a little sallow-faced fellow with sunken features, who in America one would take for a second-rate actor, but as he never says a word, and slinks away with a half frightened manner before the repast is finished, one is at a loss to decipher his calling. It will be strange if there be not at that table a portly matron with bulging jowls and an incipient moustache, who sternly eyes her meek - faced daughter and replies in guttural monosyllables to the occasional remarks of her diminutive husband. The conversation is not general, occasional remarks are addressed at random by the man of importance at the head of the table. The drummer from

Madrid tries to talk to the bride from Bilboa, but the eyes of the bridegroom twitch so excitedly that he desists and addresses a remark to the sallow-faced unknown, who replies with a sickly smile and steals away. Finally the fat old man at the head of the table discovers that you are an American, and enters into a violent discussion about American interference in Cuba. It is far from pleasant, but it makes you forget the cold and the bad food, and for a time you feel less lonesome. After all, the people are no more vulgar nor the food worse than one would find at a hotel in a western town.

Sometimes in those provincial inns you are the only guest. The waiter then beomes your companion, and when the meal is finished you have learned the gossip of the village, the names of the people of importance, the woes of the land, the peccadillos of the parish priest, and all that is of interest in the prosaic lives of the people.

The Land of the Castanet

There is little to be seen in most provincial towns beyond the streets and the people, but one who has a fondness for life and color and graceful outline, finds much to interest him at every step. There is the narrow street rambling away before you, with no apparent regard for rectilinearity, its white-walled houses shining in the sunlight, or dark in shadow, its smooth cobble stones undulated and time-worn by the tread of generations of villagers. Street urchins play in the sun, housewives loll in the doorways, patient donkeys amble by, their little bodies almost hidden by huge straw panniers filled with charcoal or shining pottery. As you saunter along you pass the door of the parish church with its inevitable coterie of beggars. The chanting of priests attracts you within, and standing there uncovered you view for a while the impressive religious scene. The church is dismal and cold, and the ghost - like figures kneeling in prayer seem not of this

A TABERNA

world. Candles glimmer on the altar, and little lamps burn dimly before the shrines of saints; the distant chapels are lost in gloom, and the air you breathe is of the tomb. From the choir comes the sombre droning of the priests, and the kneeling women mumble and cross themselves in reverence.

But the sun is shining in the street outside and the white houses and blue Spanish sky make you forget the sombre religious gloom. There is a taberna at the corner, too, and your bones have been chilled in that cold church, so you wander in and bow to the landlord and his patrons. "Una copita de aguardiente," the drink of the country, is the order you give, and while sipping the distilled anise seed, you have time to gaze about and examine the place. The room is low and dingy. There is a long counter on which the fat proprietor is leaning, and behind him are a row of casks and shelves with huge bottles of red wine. A couple of tables and some rough chairs complete

the furniture, and under the tables charcoal braziers are smouldering. Some
smooth - faced Spaniards, with broad
brimmed felt hats and graceful capas, are
huddled about the braziers drinking. You
praise the aguardiente and the garrulous
landlord proudly states that it is his own
distilling. Nothing will do but you must
see his still, so meekly following his lead
you walk through intricate byways for
perhaps half a mile to a deserted con-
vent. There in an old court, moss-
grown and crumbling, he has installed
his apparatus. It is characteristic of
laggard Spain. A charcoal fire smould-
ers under a huge earthen retort, where
the wine is boiled, and the distilling
process is completed by passing the
liquid through three coils of pipe chilled
in a tub of water. In another corner of
the court stands a primitive wine press,
worked by a huge wooden screw and a
long wooden lever weighted at one end
by stones. The proprietor is as proud
of this simple "plant" as though it were

an enormous industry with all the con-
trivances of modern skill.

On the way back to the taberna he
regales you with minute details of his
profits and business prospects, and not
satisfied with this, he must show you his
house, and the vaults where his wine is
stored. It is worth seeing, for it is typical of the country. There is a stone
paved patio or court, where the women
of the family are grinding corn, just as
the women did in the days of Moorish
Spain, and in the living rooms above you
get an idea of how a Spanish family
lives. The bedrooms are small but neat,
with red counterpanes upon the beds
and lithographs of saints upon the walls,
but space is begrudged, and in the living
room and kitchen, casks and bottles and
bunches of grapes and raisins are stored.
There is a smell of garlic and oil, and a
feeling of dampness everywhere, and
although the patio, with its graceful
arches and crumbling stairways where
clothes are drying and the women are

squatting before their corn, would attract a painter, it is not what we call homelike. One is glad to leave the odor of garlic and the dampness, and reach the street again where the sun is shining.

There is the market place, too, with its graceful Moorish colonnade and its canopied booths, its piles of yellow oranges, and festoons of garlic. Color and life are there, although the life is rather indolent, for the market men are mostly sleeping in the sun, and the donkeys blink their eyes as they stand patiently awaiting the cry of *arrhé borrico*, which summons them to toil.

The hours passed in a provincial town are lazy and dreamy, and you care not for time; but they are hours to be long remembered, for time seems to have been turned back a century at least.

You wonder, too, if the nineteenth century, with all its bustle and activity, has brought more contentment and happiness to mankind. Is not the listless

Spaniard sleeping in the sun as happy and contented as man ever is? But the philosophy of indolence is difficult to defend even from the standpoint of epicureanism, while even in those provincial towns there are monuments of activity and greatness side by side with the evidence of modern sloth. If the town be Ronda, for instance, you may lean upon the iron paling of the Alameda, and, gazing over the valley of the Guadalevin, be reminded of the prowess of the Moor, and the energy of the Spaniard in days gone by. The purple mountains stand out bold and clear against the sky, and the river dashes through the famous gorge a thousand feet below. Ancient Ronda perched upon a spur of rocks looks down upon the rushing waters; the Moorish mills are grinding corn as in the days of Hamet El Zegri, the last alcaide of Arab rule. The black river flows swiftly past the caves where Christian captives dwelt, and surges under the noble bridge above only to dash angrily against the walls of the rocky chasm and then subside into a meek and submissive stream beyond.

Unconsciously do you think of the stirring days of Moorish warfare. The alcaide Hamet El Zegri is returning with his gomeres from a raid in the vast campiñas of the duke of Medina Sidonia. Spurring his horse up a craggy height he expects to behold his fair Ronda reposing safely as when he left, but what is his consternation at seeing the white tents of a besieging army dotting the hillside, and the royal standard of Ferdinand flapping gently in the breeze. Impotent to assail such a force he smites his breast with rage, while the cannons and lombards of the royal army batter down the towers and ramparts of his beloved city. Such are the fortunes of war. And Ronda, the impregnable, falls an easy prey to the science of gunnery, then in the experimental stage of its development.

Perhaps the provincial town where you

are tarrying is stern Segovia, all ruin, all poverty, massive and austere. An aqueduct of Trajan spans the town with its three hundred granite arches, a marvelous monument of Roman skill, but an old beggar dozing beneath its walls, tells you that the devil built it in a single night to save a fair Segoviana with whom he was in love, the trouble of going down to the river for water. Of course the maiden was touched by the attention and listened to his *jardbe de pico*, or honeyed words. But Segovia, the proud hidalgo of Old Castile, did not always sleep quietly in the sun. Its silent streets once resounded with the cries of an excited mob. It was in the early days of the reign of the Emperor Charles, when the people, ever jealous of their rights, became infuriated at a submissive cortes for voting imperial grants without obtaining redress for popular grievances. Tordesillas, the representative of Segovia, being a bold and haughty man, returned to his native city to defend his

conduct, and according to custom summoned his fellow townsmen to the church
that he might give an account of his
actions in the cortes. But the multitude,
infuriated at his insolence in attempting
to justify conduct they deemed inexcus-
able, burst open the doors of the church,
and seizing Tordesillas dragged him
through the streets with curses and
insults towards the place of public execution. The dean and canons came
forth with the holy sacrament to awe the
mob; the monks in the monasteries, by
which the luckless deputy was dragged
prayed on their knees, that his life be
spared, or at least, that he be allowed
time for absolution, but without regard
for humanity or religion, they hung their
victim up head downwards on the common gibbet. That was the beginning of
the revolt of the comuneros, an impotent
attempt of the common people to overcome their masters, the nobility. It
called forth one patriot and one brave
unselfish woman in the persons of Juan

de Padilla and his courageous wife, but they fell prey to treachery, and the result was a tightening of the screws of oppression.

An instructive story might be written on the different struggles of Spaniards for the preservation of their fueros, or rights, for political liberty was known in Spain before it was in England, and the cortes antedates parliament, but in Spain during the Middle Ages, the king usurped the rights of the people, whereas in England, the people curtailed the rights of the king. But all that is mere digression, suggested by the deserted streets of Segovia, deserted except for the occasional passing of a peasant and his donkey, or the tread of a group of artillery cadets.

The royal artillery school, like most schools and prisons of Spain, is situated in one of the sequestrated convents. The cadets are dapper little fellows, in smart uniforms, who live as they please in quarters about the town, and attend the lectures and drills. The artillery vies with a few cavalry regiments as crack corps of the Spanish army, and perhaps some of your friends in Madrid have given you a line of introduction to some son or cousin, who is pursuing his studies in Segovia. You find your cadet friend living with one or two chums in one of the old houses of the town. He has his family nurse with him, who has brought him up from childhood, and who now looks tenderly after her ward during his cadet days, by brewing his coffee, mending his clothes, and making his bed. Fancy a West Point cadet with a nurse. But these young gunners are good fellows, and they invite you to luncheon, and try to amuse you to the best of their ability, by showing the school with its usual complement of desks and blackboards and physical apparatus, not to mention a museum of guns and military appliances, and they are no doubt glad when you are gone, and amuse themselves by making fun of you behind your back, as students in all lands are very much the same.

At Toledo the royal infantry school is situated, but you visit that with the governor; the drum beats, the boys stand in ranks and salute, and inwardly vote you an intruder for causing unnecessary duty. There is a lack of smartness, however, about the Spanish cadets, a laxity of discipline, which must have its effect upon the Spanish army. One would like to say much of Toledo, because it is the most typical of Spanish cities, with its Moorish walls and sombre Spanish houses piled high on a hill top, its mighty cathedral, its churches, and its ancient synagogues. No finer view is to be had in Spain than that of Toledo, cold and grey against the blue sky, with the dark Tagus rushing beneath the graceful arches of its bridges. But Toledo is the see of an archbishop and the seat of the governor of a province, so it is scarcely a provincial town, and would deserve a chapter by itself, if it were to be done even partial justice.

Perhaps the saddest provincial town one may visit is Alcalá de Henares, the birth place of Cervantes, and seat of the great university established by Cardinal Ximenes. There is not even an omnibus at the station to meet you, and you are obliged to walk along the dusty, tree-lined road which leads to the town, and find the way as best you may to the dirty Fonda del Hidalgo, where you are probably the only guest. The guide book says that the immortal Cervantes was born in a street north of the Calle Mayor, and that the site of the house is marked by an inscription let into a wall, but neither the innkeeper, the parish priest, the shopkeepers, nor the army officers strutting in the streets are able to indicate the spot. There is a miserable theatre bearing the name Cervantes and some of the inhabitants maintain that it is erected on the spot of Cervantes' house, but certainly the great humorist is as unhonored by his fellow townsmen after death as during his sad life. While a slave in Algiers he was a man of importance both feared and respected, a leader among men; but in his native Spain, merely a prophet without honor and without competence.

The great university of Alcalá, the pride of its founder, is but a ruin. A few primary scholars mumble their alphabets to a priest in its sacred halls, but the arcades are crumbling and the stones are moss-grown. There is little to recall the flourishing days of an institution which within twenty-five years of its founding sent seven thousand students forth to greet King Francis I. of France, the royal prisoner of Emperor Charles, and caused him to exclaim: "Your Ximenes has executed more than I should have dared to conceive; he has done with his single hand what in France it has taken a line of kings to accomplish."

Ximenes was a man of resources and

modern ideas. Two provisions of his university charter might bear emulation to-day. The salary of a professor was regulated by the number of his students, and his tenure of office was only for four years, when he became eligible for reappointment. There were no sinecures where stern Ximenes was master.

As Spanish trains run at unseasonable hours, sometimes starting just before dawn, when you leave a provincial town it is usually at night. But a Spanish town by night is perhaps more attractive than by day. Lamps flicker at the street corners, weird figures in flowing cloaks saunter idly by, or stand in groups discussing the events of the day. The little shops are lighted, and the articles displayed for sale assume fantastic forms, while from time to time the sereno, or night watchman, trudges by with his pike and lantern, calling forth the hour and the state of the weather. The omnibus which takes you from the fonda to the station is driven by a loquacious fellow, who prattles away to his mules and you, seemingly without distinction. The streets are filled with people, for above all things the Spaniard delights in strolling. All classes are there, old men with stooping shoulders and halting step; young gallants, matones or town bullies, priests, soldiers and beggars, passing and repassing. Smart young officers strut by with clanking swords and rattling spurs, eying the dark-eyed girls, who saunter past in groups, and from the taberna comes the hum of voices and the click of the castanet. Then as the team of mules swings into a more deserted by-way, you pass the cloaked figure of a lover earnestly whispering at some window, and hearing the half suppressed ripple of a woman's laugh, you know that the damsel behind the bars has been the recipient of extravagant words of love. Perhaps the clatter of the mules disturbs the song of a solitary guitarist who is gazing upwards toward a balcony, for at night the Andalusian swain of whatever degree is pelando el pavo, plucking the turkey, as they call their window love-making there in the south. Then silent streets with darkened houses are reached and the lumbering omnibus rattles on into the night. In the distance down the long straight roadway where poplars rise against the black sky, the lights of the railway station glimmer faintly.

The provincial town has been left behind, sleeping as it has slept for a full century, unmindful of time, caring naught for the onward march of progress, but above all, seemingly content with its humble lot.

UNA BAILERINA

The Common People

THE redeeming feature of the Spanish nation is the common people. Howsoever much one may condemn the rulers or despise the priesthood, the lowly Spaniard, in spite of his many faults, commands respect. He has a democratic air about him, a sort of mingling of civility with a sense of equality which is very fascinating, and the more one sees of him the more difficult it is to understand how a people with such a peasantry should occupy so secondary a place among the nations. The Spaniard is certainly a patient creature, else he would not have endured so much. Perhaps he is a philosopher and realizes that in poverty lies the true solution of happiness. To have nothing, and to want nothing, certainly robs life of the greater portion of its worries. Evidently the lowly Spaniard believes thoroughly in the maxim that sufficient unto the day is the evil thereof, for he goes through life with a patience and a cheerfulness which are refreshing. Only in Barcelona, where he has been tainted with modern unrest, does he seem to fret, and with rare irony he throws aside his air of contented humility to become an anarchist. But the Catalan has never been a true Spaniard.

One must turn to the wind-swept plains of Castile, or better still, to sunny Andalusia, to find the true son of the soil. The Castilian, like his land, is sombre and cold. He is self-contained and proud, and although he walks abroad with an air of equality, not to say superiority to his fellowmen, he is apt to be morose and unbending. He does not open up his heart, and when he smiles it is with a forbidding air of reserve. The Galician, or even the Navarrese, is a far better fellow; but to

find the Spaniard at his best one must
turn to fair Andalusia. There all is
cheerful and bright; the sun is ever
shining and the castanet is clicking, the
girls are ever smiling, and the gallants
under the balconies sigh and whisper
words of love with an ardor which is
truly of the south. The Andalusian is a
child of nature, who breathes the free air
of heaven as though it belonged to him.
He is impulsive and natural, and he
walks with a careless swing which is at
once jaunty and self-respecting. His
morals may not be all that one might
ask, but his manners are the best in the
world. He has just enough of courtliness not to be oppressive, and just
enough of familiarity not to breed contempt. He respects himself, and consequently other people respect him. Unlike the Castilian, he unburdens his
heart to a stranger and makes you feel
at once at your ease. All that he asks
is to be treated as a man. Offer him a
cigarette and be he the humblest of beg-

gars, he will receive it in a manner that assures you of friendliness tempered by respect, but brush him aside with an air of contempt and he will leave no means untried to make your life uncomfortable.

English travelers whose manner toward servants is invariably overbearing, do not find themselves well served in Spain; but no servants in the world are more considerate of your wishes, more attentive to your wants, than those of the Peninsula, if they are treated as though they are human. A friendly word or a smile goes further than a handful of silver.

It may seem rather familiar, even to an American, to have the waiter who serves you in a restaurant, stand behind your chair smoking a cigarette, but that is purely a matter of custom. It might also appear objectionable to have the waiter at your hotel enter into the conversation while he is serving you, but he does this rarely, and then only with a desire to impart some bit of information or correct an erroneous impression he chances to overhear. He realizes that he is human, but unlike some of his American prototypes, he does not become obtrusive with an overbearing manner of equality, not to say superiority.

The Spaniard has been misgoverned for so many centuries that he has grown to look upon the government as a legitimate prey. The government defrauds him; therefore he will defraud the government when the opportunity presents itself. He is consequently by nature a smuggler. In addition to the national custom house at all seaports, and the frontier, each city has its own octroi, so that the temptation and the opportunity to smuggle are unusually great. Tobacco, being a government monopoly, is the popular contraband, and in spite of the carbineers who swarm along the coast, and the fleet of coast guard ships, the inhabitants of the seaport towns do not appear to have much difficulty in evading the authorities. Their methods are at times rather brazen. For instance, on leaving Algeciras which, owing to its proximity to free trade Gibraltar, is a nest of smugglers, the conductor of the train entered the compartment, and after glancing about with a mysterious air, he lifted the cushions of the seats and proceeded to fill his pockets with packages of tobacco, which had been put in a first-class carriage as the place least likely to be investigated by the authorities. On being asked if he was not afraid of detection he said that he was perfectly safe at the hands of first-class travelers, because they were invariably gentlemen. The offer of a contraband Egyptian cigarette doubly reassured him, and as fellow smugglers we sat down and smoked together. He had been a conductor of the line since its opening a few years ago, and had carried on quite a thriving contraband trade. At each station he disappeared, only to return again to refill his pockets.

In this manner his stock was disposed of to confederates all along the line from Algeciras to Ronda.

The carbineers, too, judging by the avidity with which they pass one's baggage when no one is looking, must share the profits of many a contraband transaction. Such peculation, however, is not confined to Spain. There are some Spanish officials who are incorruptible and those in places where their example should prove most salutary; that is to say in the prisons. One remembers visiting some half dozen prisons in different Spanish cities, and each time the accompanying guard, though his salary was but a pittance, politely though reluctantly refused a fee for his trouble, by saying that receiving gratuities was absolutely prohibited.

It is the custom for the waiters in the hotels to pool their tips. All the fees are turned into a common fund and shared at the end of the month. You therefore do not tip individual waiters, but on leaving the hotel you give the head waiter a sum to be divided among them all. At the hotel in Granada there was a waiter who remembered the writer from a former visit fourteen years before, and who was at the same time unusually attentive. Desiring to give the man a special reward which should not be shared with the others, he was presented with a separate sum and requested not to divide it with his fellow servants. At the time of leaving the hotel, when the waiters were gathered together to receive their conventional tip, this over-honest servant told the others that he had already received a sum apart, which he felt in duty bound to contribute to the general fund. It might be added that he was a widower with seven young children.

Spain is probably the most conservative nation in Europe. Outside the larger cities the country has been at a standstill for centuries. The ploughing is still done with wooden plows, the wheat is threshed with flails, the wine is preserved in goat skins. The arriero still trudges beside his string of mules, livening his weary way with song as he did in the days of Don Quixote, and the ventero greets the traveler at the wayside inn and regales him with the gossip of the neighborhood just as his sires have done for centuries. The court of the posada is still crowded with huge high carts, and the muleteers, huddled about a charcoal brazier, sip their aguardiente, while the sereno trudges past with his lantern and pike calling forth the hour and the state of the weather.

The common people of Spain are so unlike those of other nations; they are so thoroughly the children of the soil, untainted by contact with the world, that a lover of the picturesque is apt to overlook, in his enthusiasm for their artistic qualities, the fact that they must be slothful and ambitionless to be contented with their stagnate existence. It is perhaps unfair to call them slothful, for they work faithfully and long, but

they eschew machinery, and ask no better lot than that of their fathers.

The laboring classes in other countries
are apt to look askance upon their superiors and treat them with suspicion, but
the Spanish artizan will invite you to
share his sour wine or coarse bread without the slightest hesitation. He will
talk with you as man to man, and yet
without a semblance of disrespect.
Chancing to enter a Sevillian pottery on
New Year's morning one heard the sound
of voices and the click of castanets in
the court beyond. The proprietor ex-
plained that he was giving his workmen
a little entertainment in honor of the
day, and extended an invitation to par-
ticipate in the festivities. Gathered in
the court were some thirty potters
dressed in holiday attire. The proprietor's daughter was dancing the graceful
Sevillana with one of her father's workmen, and her mother was dispensing
cakes and aguardiente to the gathering.
The employees were singing and keep-

A DANCING GIRL

ing time to the dancing by clapping their
hands, and one has never seen more
happy and contented faces than those
Sevillian workmen presented that New
Year's morning.

The entrance of a strange foreigner
might appear a source of embarrass-
ment, but on the contrary each person
present greeted one with a friendly smile
and a word of welcome. Aguardiente
was offered, and we all clicked glasses
and drank each other's healths as though
we had been life-long friends. Dances
and songs followed in quick succession.
There were some clever comedians
among those humble potters. One in
particular, a fat little chap with a face
like Coquelin's, might have won fame
on any stage. His grimaces were con-
vulsing, and he had a quaint humor which
was irresistible. He was the popular
favorite, and his songs were greeted
with great applause. A glass of aguardiente handed by the pretty daughter of
the house was sufficient to produce an

encore, and as each song had the additional inspiration of another glass they grew more amusing and more ribald as the performance progressed.

One song, called La Monjita, or little nun, he prefaced with an address delivered in solemn, priest-like tones, running somewhat as follows: " Ladies, gentlemen and distinguished Yankees, I will now sing you a song which I alone am capable of rendering. Others may whistle the refrain but no one else can remember the words. In fact I do not remember them myself, but having a ready wit I am able to supply the deficiency at a moment's notice. The like of this song has never been heard in Triana, or even Seville, and no singer of the Cervantes theatre can compete with my vocal talent. Were I not too serious and virtuous a person to sing upon the stage my pockets would to-day be overflowing with dollars, and the public upon their knees before me. This song I will sing in the language of old Andalusia, which no one here can understand but in order that its rare humor may not escape the audience entirely I will sing each alternate verse in English.''

Then he began singing a humorous but indelicate account of the adventures of a young nun, seemingly without the least regard for the presence of the proprietor's wife and daughter. At the end of each stanza he solemnly announced that the next verse would be sung in English.

There were others, too, who added to the merriment. One little old weazen-faced Celtiberian, with an Irish cast of countenance, who had been lulled to sleep in the corner by the fumes of aguardiente, suddenly awoke and insisted upon dancing the tango. His slow, precise movements, to a dance requiring unusual agility, were most comical.

When the entertainment was over we drank again, and shook hands all around, calling each other friend and brother, all in a feeling of pure good

fellowship.   But wherever you chance
to meet a party of merrymakers in Andalusia the reception is the same; you are
invited to share their food and drink,
and if you unbend and meet them half
way your reception is so cordial and sincere that you are tempted to believe
that nowhere is the spirit of thorough
good fellowship so rife as among the
common people of Spain.

The women of the people, too, are more
attractive than those of the aristocracy.
There is a piquancy and dash about
them which is refreshing.   Their voices
are harsh, but their black eyes are filled
with fire, and the poise of their heads
gives them an air of coquettish defiance.
They are fond of color and seldom fail
to wear a red rose caught in their glossy
hair.   The hair and the feet of Spanish
girls of the lower classes are invariably
neat.   They wear dainty shoes, and their
meager wages are squandered on elaborate coiffures.   They are contented with a
calico gown and a gay colored shawl

about their shoulders, but they are always well booted, and their hair is arranged in the latest French mode.

Dancing is the favorite pastime of the Andalusian, and the dancing girls of Seville, Cadiz and Malaga are found all over Spain. There are the gypsies, too, but their dancing is but a vulgar variety of the movements of their Gwazee prototypes of Egypt. The Sevillana, however, is lithe and graceful, and the dance which bears her name is free from the sensuous movements of other dances, such as the tango, so popular in the lower class of cafés chantants. Each city in the south of Spain has its particular dance, such as the baile de Malaga, etc. There are special dances, too, like the baile Manchera, the Soleada, the Fandango, etc. Some for one person, some in which two (a man and a girl) face each other and dance a paso doble, or others like the Fandango, in which a number take part. In none of them, however, do the dancers join arms as in waltzing, and invariably the movements of the arms play as important a part as those of the feet.

The girls who dance in the cafés are professionals, paid for their work, but they enter into the spirit of the dancing as though they enjoyed it. Between the dances they leave the stage and mix with the audience. When they see a stranger they come and take a seat at your table and ask for a glass of manzanilla. They are very naïve and artless, and full of life, and talk of nothing but their art. Their morality, though not unimpeachable, is not open to the charge of sordidness. Spaniards say that although each one has her "querido," he is always a man of the people, and that the advances of wealthy libertines are almost invariably repelled.

Dancing, however, is not confined to the women of Spain; the men are often their equals, if not their superiors. They are lighter on their feet, more agile in their movements. Without exception

the best dancing one saw in Spain was
an unpremeditated baile arranged on
the spur of the moment. A party of us
were breakfasting on Christmas morning
at a suburban café in Seville; a couple
of clever guitarists had been called in to
play the national music. When breakfast was over and we were smoking our
cigarettes, one of the musicians suggested a dance, and said that the waiter
was no mean performer. The waiter,
a typical Andalusian, with clean cut
features and a slight agile figure, who performed his labor in his shirt sleeves and
with a cigarette between his lips, pro-
tested with becoming modesty, that he
was only a tyro, but that our cabman
waiting outside was a " Bailarin " of
great prowess. So cabby was summoned
from his perch on the box, and after being well fortified with a glass or two of
the wine of Jerez, he and the waiter proceeded to dance the whole gamut of Andalusian dances, the rest of us keeping
time with our hands in true Spanish fash-

ion.   The cabman was indeed a marvel. Never has one seen better dancing; he was graceful and lithe, and his movements had the finish of a professional ballet dancer. He threw his whole heart into his work, and seemed ready to continue indefinitely. The waiter, too, was a good foil, as he had much of the dry humor of Andalusia.   He interpolated droll remarks, and between the dances regaled us with characteristic songs of the people. The whole affair was so impromptu, so thoroughly typical of the country, that as a performance it was superior to the best efforts of paid professionals.

To one familiar with the tenements of the larger American cities, a Spanish tenement house, or "casa de vecinos," (house of neighbors) as it is called, seems a veritable paradise. Not that there are no evidences of squalor and poverty, for dirt is plentiful, and the Spanish poor are poorer than our own, but the corral, as these tenements are

CASA DE VECINOS

sometimes called, has plenty of good air
and sunshine, and the surroundings are
attractive to the eye. The corral has
the usual open court surrounded by a
double arcade. The tenements open
onto this court, and the Andalusian poor
man, instead of gazing down a narrow
filthy city street, looks from his doorway
upon clean white-washed walls and growing palms. There is the blue sky above
to cheer him, and a fountain trickles in
the courtyard. Birds chirp in their
cages, and bright-eyed girls loiter by the
fountain. From an artistic standpoint
the casa de vecinos leaves little to be
desired. Who would think of painting
a New York tenement? However, the
quarters are small, and the smells are
not of the sweetest, and after all, the life
of the poor the world over is much the
same. But if any choice is to be made
the poor Spaniard's lot has much to com-
mend. His wants are little and his
diversions many; his eye is ever glad-
dened by green trees and graceful out-

lines, and his heart is not disturbed by wild political theories. His religion is the best religion for the poor man, because it holds out hope and commands fear, and by its church organization and tenets teaches obedience and respect for organized society.

But if one wants to come face to face with misery, the prison is the place to find it. The lot of the Spanish prisoner is miserable in the extreme. The writer visited six or seven prisons in different cities, and with the exception of the carcel modelo, or model prison, in Madrid, and the women's prison at Alcalá, found them loathsome dens, where the miserable prisoners are huddled together in filth. A description of the Seville prison will suffice, as that institution is typical of the rest. The building is an old monastery, converted to its present use by placing iron bars on the windows and sentry boxes about the walls. There are not more than half a dozen employees to look after five hundred malefactors, so the prisoners are left very much to their own resources. The only labor which is compulsory is the domestic labor of the establishment, and that is poorly performed. The cloisters reek with filth, and the prisoners themselves are a ragged dirty lot, who huddle together in the sun without even the solace of hard work. They sleep on straw mattresses spread on the stone floors, and their two daily meals consist of rice and beans, and a small loaf of bread. They are permitted to smoke if fortunate enough to possess friends on the outside willing to supply the necessary tobacco. Clothes are not provided, although in the penitentiaries, for longer term sentences, a coarse brown uniform is furnished the inmates. In the Sevillian prison, however, the prisoners are arrayed in any form of tattered garment they can obtain.

Looking down from an upper window upon the throng of prisoners eating their morning meal in the open court yard, one could not help thinking that no matter what his surroundings may be, the Spaniard is attractive to the eye. The poor creatures were squatting on the floor in groups of from ten to twelve. In the centre of each group was an earthen pot filled with the routine mixture of rice and beans. They had no plates or forks, and only a very few were fortunate enough to possess a spoon. All were hurriedly reaching into the common pot, and gobbling their food at a pace which betrayed the natural fear that the faster eaters might obtain an undue proportion of the miserable repast. But in spite of the misery and filth the grouping was picturesque, the costuming attractive, and above the white prison walls was the blue Andalusian sky.

The prisoners are allowed to receive gifts of food and clothes, and to converse with their friends through an iron grille. Liquor of course is forbidden, and many are the devices adopted by solicitous friends for smuggling aguardiente beyond the bars. The civil director of the institution presented the writer with an interesting collection of double-bottomed pots and cans, which, ostensibly filled with food, had contained the precious liquor in their concealed compartments. Some of them were very ingeniously constructed; likewise some knives made from the handles of spoons, and other objects turned to illegitimate use. The great fault of Spanish prisons is that the prisoners are not compelled to work, and are given free intercourse among themselves; thus criminals of all sorts are thrown together, and the better elements are dragged down to the level of the worst. That the Spanish authorities realize this is evidenced by the model prison of Madrid, where each prisoner has his cell and silence is imposed during the first period of the incarceration. The model prison is well named, for it is a model of its kind, admirably constructed and scrupulously clean; but even there labor is not enforced, although permitted.

Sociology, however, is far from the purpose of this little book, and crime and its devotees are repulsive, even when attired in the graceful garb of the Spaniard.

It is an unfortunate thing for Spain, and perhaps the secret of its misfortunes, that it does not possess a middle class. Between the patrician and the peasant there is only the petty shopkeeper. Even he is not thrifty and frugal like the French bourgeois. If he is fortunate enough to acquire a competence, his son, instead of continuing the family business, must be a soldier or a government clerk, in order that he may purge the family of the taint of trade.

The Spanish bourgeois is certainly repulsive. Lacking the courtliness of the nobility, and the easy grace of the peasant, he is in every sense a coarse, boorish fellow, slovenly and uncleanly, whose manners are execrable, and whose character has not even the redeeming feature of thrift. He is ignorant, bigoted and

SPANISH GYPSIES

lazy, and the more one sees of Spain the more strongly one feels convinced that the expulsion of the Jews and Moors, the thrifty and producing classes, laid the foundation of nineteenth century poverty. Spain has never had a true middle class since the Moor and the Jew were banished. The gulf between the nobility and the peasantry is too great. The poor are hopelessly poor, with no chance to rise. The nobility are too closely bound by pride and tradition to descend to work; and there is no energetic middle class to develop the splendid resources of the land. The bigoted Isabella and the imbecile Philip little knew the injury they were doing their beloved land when in the name of religion they banished hundreds of thousands of the most useful of their subjects.

Gibraltar

LIKE a lion couchant, slumbering with his shaggy head between his paws, lies ponderous Gibraltar. Waves splash lazily at its feet, fleecy clouds drift peacefully above its scraggy form, the warships of Europe ride pigmy-like at anchor beneath its towering sides; while puffing launches and swarms of white-winged feluccas dart to and fro between the rocky monster and the Spanish shore. Ships pass and repass, men of many nations come and go, the world moves on; yet silently this lion of England watches, the ever ready, ever alert, guardian of the Mediterranean.

That is one's first impression of Gibraltar, when approaching from the sea; but as the ship draws nearer, and the cable rattles in the hawse-hole, the scene

is changed to one of life and action.
Boats crowd about the steamer, ruffianly
watermen jabber and gesticulate, whistles screech, and the faint notes of a
bugle, or the roll of drums come from
distant barrack yards. Perched in clus-
ters along the water-front are the stuccoed houses of the Spanish town; beyond and stretching far out into the
Mediterranean, the dull grey walls of
ramparts and batteries, with here and
there, and almost everywhere, little
specks of red, marking the sentries on
their beats.

Gibraltar is no longer a lion, but a
monster hive of humanity, with its rocky
sides honeycombed with galleries and
casemates, where scarlet bees swarm,
and dull drones toil. Through the years
they have labored with chisel and blast;
patiently and wisely they have built
their hive, and woe to the bear who at-
tempts to crush them; he will feel their
sting.

How alien, how cosmopolitan is this

The Land of the Castanet

Gibraltar, a mere spur of rock, sticking like a thorn in the side of Spain, and yet not Spanish, or Moorish, or British, but rather a sourish leaven of Spaniard and Moor, with red English plums, dotted here and there, to give it a zest and flavor not its own. One forgets what a thoroughly detestable fellow the "rock scorpion" is, what an offscouring, without nationality, individuality or friend. The Spaniard despises the natives of "Gib," the Englishman scorns them, the stranger distrusts them, yet there are some twenty thousand of them, living there under martial rule, their actions regulated, their laws made and executed by a foreign power. A very good thing for them, too, as they are made to behave themselves, and keep themselves —or at least their streets—clean in a way that is unknown in neighboring Spain.

But the "rock scorpion" in all his entirety, is not to be seen from a steamer's deck. One must land at the water port and patiently await the arrival of one's luggage to realize what a thorough blending of the east and west, time and foreign conquest have made of the Rock of Tarik.

No more cosmopolitan scene is to be witnessed in Europe than that presented at the water port. It is an ever-shifting panorama of strange humanity.

Olive-skinned watermen, with half-burned cigarettes between their lips, doze on the thwarts of their high-prowed boats, while swarthy peasants from Algeciras or Linea, with brilliant sashes and broad-brimmed hats, skin-tight trousers, and short braided jackets, come and go with the lazy air of Spain. Low-wheeled vans freighted with English beer or Chicago beef, rattle over the cobbles of the quay, while mules with jangling bells and gaily embroidered headstalls, struggle in the shafts of high-wheeled Spanish carts, and patient donkeys, their little bodies smothered beneath bulging panniers of straw, trot by unmindful of the shrill cries of their masters.

The Land of the Castanet

What color; what variety! There are stately Moors with flowing robes of white, and high-bound turbans; thin savage Riffians, sleek padres with shovel hats and sombre gowns, dark-eyed women from Andalusia, their oily hair gracefully adorned with lace mantillas; barefooted urchins, tourists, stevedores, policemen, sailors of all nations, and soldiers of Spain, with smart Tommy Atkins, sturdy and erect, as only the British soldiers can be, standing guard over all.

The morning is calm and misty, not a ripple on the water, not a breath on the folds of the drying sails. Behind the gates and ramparts of the town the huge rock rises against the sky like the painted curtain of a theatre, its grey side studded with little houses, square and white as the toy houses of children, with here and there upon the hillsides tufts of scrubby foliage, cold and gaunt as the rock itself. Then, as the sun breaks through the mist, dew sparkles on the green grass of the ramparts, the bayonets of the sentries glisten, smoke curls from the chimneys of the town, flags flutter, the colors on the hillside grow warm and brilliant, and the stirring notes of the fifes and drums break on the morning air.

But that is only the landing stage, where the boats land from the ships at anchor in the bay. The town itself stretches along the western side of the rock for a mile or more in a series of narrow streets, where English signs and Spanish houses are mixed incongruously; where Englishmen and Spaniards meet, but do not affiliate.

There are the same stuccoed houses that one sees in Spain, white or delicate blue and yellow; the same graceful balconies and sloping roofs of tile, the same dingy little shops open to the street, the same bodegas at the corner, where groups of loiterers are gathered, drinking valdepeñas or aguardiente, and all without the filth and many of the smells.

The Land of the Castanet

The English keep the town clean; they place English names upon the street corners; English signs and English goods are seen on every hand; red-coated English soldiers and red-faced English matrons mingle with the crowds which throng the streets; but the town and the people are as Spanish to-day as they were when the Prince of Darmstadt and Sir George Rooke attacked the rock by land and sea, and added another fortress to the spoils of England.

That was in 1704, during the war of the Spanish succession, when Spain was weak and imbecile, and all Europe was fighting for her crown. The garrison scarcely mustered a hundred men, but even this handful might have held out had it not been for some patron saint, whose festival happened to fall on the second day of the bombardment. The garrison thinking devotion the better part of valor, went to pray, and the place was surprised by scaling the eastern portion of the rock and attacking the fortress from above. When the captors entered the town Darmstadt hoisted the Spanish standard, and proclaimed King Charles, but the admiral, with the voracity of the true Englishman, took possession in the name of the Queen of England.

It was a game of grab, not the only one nor the last which England has played, but it was successful, and there the red-coats have remained for nearly two centuries, by no other right than that of possession. In the meantime the Spanish officers at Linea date their letters from Gibraltar, with the parenthetical remark, that it is temporarily in the possession of the English, and Tommy Atkins, pacing his beat, gazes disdainfully across the barren strip of neutral ground at the dark-skinned sentries who guard the Spanish lines.

It was somewhere near this neutral ground, that Tarik, the one-eyed Moor, landed at the foot of the rock of Calpe, as the "Gib" was then called, when he came in the year 711, with his little army of Arabs and Berbers to reconnoitre Gothic Spain. Tarik's master, Mousa, the vali of Arab Tingitana, across the straits, had sent his one-eyed general, with an army of light horsemen, to burn and pillage, and then return to Africa, but the wily veteran saw the defenceless state of the enervated kingdom. Advancing boldly into Andalusia, he met King Roderic on the banks of the Guadalete near Jerez, and in spite of every disadvantage in numbers, position and supplies, he routed the effeminate army of the Goth and overran Spain. Tarik incurred the jealousy of Mousa, his chief. Conquest after conquest followed. The Moor in Spain is but a memory, but the name of the one-eyed victor still remains, where the conqueror of a later day looks down from the rock of Calpe upon the sunny plains and snow-capped siena of Andalusia. Gibel Tarik, meaning hill of Tarik, has been corrupted by successive ages and tongues into Gibraltar.

Gibraltar

All that is history, and of history there is a surfeit at the "Gib." There have been sieges and stormings galore, but the one the English most revere is the defense of "Old Eliot' in 1779, when for four years the rock held out against the united arms of France and Spain, and in spite of the floating batteries of d'Arcon, which "could neither be burnt, sunk nor taken," it still remains a British possession, garrisoned by a British force of six thousand men.

One confesses to a fondness for this British force. Wherever the English soldier finds his home there is color, life and smartness. With his forage cap perched aslant upon his close cropped head, his brilliant tunic buttoned to the chin with shining buttons of brass, his pipe clayed belt, and his "swagger stick," he walks the street with a mingled sturdiness and dash quite his own. His face is bronzed, and his hair is flaxen, his shoulders are broad and his eyes are keen, and seeing him one understands the remark of Napoleon, that "the British infantry is the best in the world; thank God there are so few of them."

Gibraltar might be said to be in a continuous state of siege. The vigorous rules of a military post are never relaxed. The fact that it is a foreign post, held by force in a foreign country, is never forgotten. At retreat the gates are closed; at reveille they are opened. None but Englishmen are allowed to enter without a pass, and none but residents permitted to spend the night. The Spanish laborers from San Roque who come for the day are forced to leave at nightfall. A bell of warning clangs like an alarm of fire before retreat is sounded, and then the streets are thronged with grimy workmen from Spain—men, women, even children, hurrying to get beyond the gates before the closing of the town.

At sunset the warden bearing the keys, marches through the streets to the stirring strains of the fifes and drums or the braying notes of Highland pipes, and locks the gates for the night. Again at the hour of taps, martial music echoes through the town, as the pipers of the Black watch or the drummers of some regiment of the line, swing through the narrow streets, their red coats glinting in the lights which glare from shop or tavern, their feet falling in measured time upon the glistening cobbles of the pavement.

At night a city is at its best or worst according to one's point of view. Then the noises of the day are gone, the dirt is invisible, and harsh outlines or inharmonious colors are lost in sombre shadow. Gibraltar at night becomes completely Spanish. Men wrapped in the folds of graceful capas fill the streets, saunter idly in pairs or groups, unmindful of the existence of sidewalks; women and girls, with colored shawls of brilliant hues and mantillas on their comely heads, chatter and laugh in

the tones of Andalusia, while glasses
chink in the bodegas, and from behind
closed doors comes the click of castanets, the twang of a guitar. There are
dingy highways, too, winding upward
into the night, where paupers skulk, or
dark skinned Cyprians squat in their
doorways and cast languishing glances
at stalwart Tommy Atkins, as he loiters
toward the barrack yard.

In the main street is the "Café Universal,"where at night the soldiers of the
garrison and sailors of the fleets gather
to drink their English beer; and natives
of the town who ape their English masters assemble about the marble tables
to chat and talk and pretend to be English. These anglomaniacs of the "Gib"
are a curious type,—they must be despised by both Spaniard and Briton, but
they persevere in wearing covert coats,
and English caps, in carrying bamboo
sticks, and talking English with a soft
lisp which is unmistakable. They are
fond of fox terriers and brilliant ties,

and the Café Universal seems to be their lounging place.   This café is well named. It is the universal meeting ground of all classes of "Gib" society.   The arms of many nations are painted on the walls where mirrors glisten, and the advertisements of Bass's Ale and Canadian whiskey, American hotels, or Spanish wines, mingle in cosmopolite confusion. There is a din of voices, the air is dense with smoke, canary birds chirp in their gilded cages, waiters of Spanish cast come and go or loiter by the tables, smoking their cigarillos with a familiarity which is truly Spanish; while here and there, mingling, with the dull black of civilian dress, are the dashing uniforms of the British soldiers, and at a table by themselves, a group of blue jackets from a Yankee cruiser, now half seas over, to remind one of the land across the ocean.   Above the hum of voices rise the notes of a piano, while upon a platform placed to one side, dark girls from Malaga, dressed à la manola, with brilliant scarfs of silk and roses in their hair, dance to the time of castanets, the sensuous dances of Southern Spain.

But all that is of the town and people, and the guide book says the town is uninteresting and dull.   One forgets the mighty rock which towers above, frowning and grey, with its old Moorish castle perched like an eagle on a crag, with its chilly galleries chiseled and blasted in the limestone, where the mouths of cannons glare yawning from behind the cactus or palmetto, and the steps of the sentry echo.   Scrambling through a rocky port one gazes down for full a thousand feet upon the harbor and the plain below.   Dwarfish ships ride at anchor on the bay; a battalion, at extended order drill, is spread over the parade like little tufts of red upon a carpet of green velvet.   Beyond are the race course and polo grounds where little ponies scramble like mice at play, and then the narrow strip of neutral land stretches between the sea and the bay, where sentries pace and the sturdy Briton gazes defiantly at the sunburnt child of Spain. In the distance, across the blue water, the white walls of Algeciras and San Roque shine in the sunlight, and the green sloping hills and snow-capped mountains of Andalusia rise sharp against the fleecy sky. It is a view to be remembered.

The batteries of ponderous modern guns, and El Hacho, the signal tower, are now closed to visitors, so one no longer gazes, as at a former visit, across the straits to the misty hills of Morocco where the Moorish cities of Tangier and Ceuta nestle by the sea. You used to scramble on donkeys over the crest of the rock, and visit St. Michael's cave below; cockney gunners used to point the great guns at Africa, and detail their carrying power and caliber, but the authorities have grown suspicious, and now but half the "Gib" is shown to the foreign visitor, while even the whereabouts of the newest batteries is kept a secret.

After a visit to the galleries tunneled in the northern face of the rock, where antiquated cannon point in mere bravado toward the Spanish lines, you drive along the ledge-like road which runs a zig-zag way to the Alameda. Beside this road are perched the dainty little villas of the officers; trim Spanish houses, with English garden spots, behind grey walls of stone, where roses bloom and there is a sweet smell of jasmine. Neat English maids and ruddy English babies, smart pony carts and basket phaetons with Spanish servants in London liveries, remind one of foggy England. Here healthy girls with flat-soled boots and pink-faced officers in "mufti" stride along with a swinging step in striking contrast to the sauntering Spaniard. But there are the strings of meek-eyed donkeys with their swaying ears and the tinkling goat bells to recall the south, and then the Alameda with its palms and cactus plants is reached. A park with geraniums and bowers, and tropical trees laid out with the precision of the English landscape gardener, this Alameda is the pride of Gibraltar. But there is only time for a glance at the shady paths and green waters for the spry Gibraltar pony is scrambling over the ground, and soon the little phaeton-like cab is whirling through the streets of the town again. Huge bastions with frowning guns— barrack yards, where soldiers lounge upon the balconies—military storehouses —the governor's mansion, and tortuous lines of narrow street way, with quaint smoky houses and sloping roofs, pass in review. You meet Spanish "bobbies" in English clothes, and Spanish boys in Eton jackets, diminutive car-like 'buses with jangling bells upon the horses necks, huge carts drawn by oxen or mules, smart officers astride their Eng-

lish mounts, and countless other sights,
and then the show is over; the hotel is
reached.

From a former visit of much longer
duration, there are memories to add of
officers' messes and clubs, tennis parties, dinners and visits, for an English
garrison always makes a charming
society. But all that is no more typical of the "Gib" than it is of Halifax, of
Malta, or wherever the Union Jack is
unfurled.

The last glimpse of Gibraltar was
from Algeciras across the bay. From
there the rock looks as peaceful and
sleepy as the fishermen who dozed in
their boats.

A Carabinero, mounting guard, marched lazily to and fro upon the quay. His
timeworn uniform was ill-fitting, his beard
unshaven, but he was picturesque and
typical of sunny Spain. He blended
with the feluccas and the brigantines
—the beggars and the white washed

houses, and made it difficult to realize
that across that stretch of water, where
the white sails glared in the sun-light
was a mighty fortress, with bastions and
guns, with galleries and batteries, where
the flag of England fluttered and the
Highlander was piping the war-songs
of his island home.

PRINTED AT THE LAKESIDE PRESS
FOR HERBERT S. STONE & CO.
PUBLISHERS, CHICAGO

Catalogue
of
The Publications
of
Herbert S. Stone & Company

The Caxton Building,

Chicago.

To be had of all Booksellers, or will be sent postpaid on receipt of price by the Publishers.

HENRY JAMES.
WHAT MAISIE KNEW; a novelette. 16mo. $1.25.

The announcement of a new book by Mr. James is in itself an event of no slight literary importance. The present volume represents his latest work and is worthy the attention of all persons interested in English and American letters.

RICHARD Le GALLIENNE.

PROSE FANCIES; second series, by the author of "The Book-bills of Narcissus," etc., with a cover designed by Frank Hazenplug. 16mo. $1.25.

"In these days of Beardsley pictures and decadent novels, it is good to find a book as sweet, as pure, as delicate as Mr. Le Gallienne's."—NEW ORLEANS PICAYUNE.

"PROSE FANCIES ought to be in everyone's summer library, for it is just the kind of a book one loves to take to some secluded spot to read and dream over."—KANSAS CITY TIMES.

"There are witty bits of sayings by the score, and sometimes whole paragraphs of nothing but wit. Somewhere there is a little skit about 'Scotland, the country that takes its name from the whisky made there,' and the transposed proverb like : 'It is an ill wind for the shorn lamb,' and 'Many rise on the stepping stones of their dead relations,' are brilliant. 'Most of us would never be heard of were it not for our enemies,' is a capital epigram."—CHICAGO TIMES-HERALD.

"Mr. Le Gallienne is first of all a poet, and these little essays, which savor somewhat of Lamb, of Montaigne, of Lang, and of Birrell, are larded with verse of exquisite grace. He rarely ventures into the grotesque, but his fancy follows fair paths; a certain quaintness of expression and the idyllic atmosphere of the book charm one at the beginning and carry one through the nineteen 'fancies' that comprise the volume."—CHICAGO RECORD.

MARIA LOUISE POOL.

IN BUNCOMBE COUNTY. 16mo. $1.25.

A volume of connected sketches of country life in the South. It is on the order of Miss Pool's recent book entitled "In a Dike Shanty" which received such favorable comment. It is not sensational; it is not exciting; it is merely peaceful and pleasing, with a quiet current of delightful humor running all through.

MARTIN J. PRITCHARD.

WITHOUT SIN; a novel. 12mo. $1.25.
Second edition.

The New York Journal gave a half-page review of the book and proclaimed it "the most startling novel yet."

"Abounds in situations of thrilling interest. A unique and daring book."—Review of Reviews (London).

"One is hardly likely to go far wrong in predicting that Without Sin will attract abundant notice. Too much can scarcely be said in praise of Mr. Pritchard's treatment of his subject."— Academy (London).

"The very ingenious way in which improbable incidents are made to appear natural, the ingenious manner in which the story is sustained to the end, the undoubted fascination of the writing, and the convincing charm of the principal characters, are just what make this novel so deeply dangerous while so intensely interesting."—The World (London).

CHAP-BOOK STORIES; a volume of Reprints from the Chap-Book, by Octave Thanet, Grace Ellery Channing, Maria Louise Pool, and others. 16mo. $1.25.

The authors of this volume are all American. Beside the well-known names, there are some which were seen in the Chap-Book for the first time. The volume is bound in an entirely new and startling fashion.

CHAP-BOOK ESSAYS, by T. W. Higginson, Louise Chandler Moulton, H. H. Boyesen, H. W. Mabie, and others. 16mo. $1.25.

Essays, by the most distinguished living writers, which it has been judged worth preserving in more permanent form than the issues of the Chap-Book could give.

ALBERT KINROSS.

THE FEARSOME ISLAND; being a Modern rendering of the narrative of one Silas Fordred, Master Mariner of Hythe, whose shipwreck and subsequent adventures are herein set forth. Also an appendix accounting in a rational manner for the seeming marvels that Silas Fordred encountered during his sojourn on the fearsome island of Don Diego Rodriguez. With a cover designed by Frank Hazenplug. 16mo. $1.25.

GABRIELE D'ANNUNZIO.

EPISCOPO AND COMPANY. Translated by Myrta Leonora Jones. 16mo. $1.25.

Gabriele d'Annunzio is the best known and most gifted of modern Italian novelists. His work is making a great sensation at present in all literary circles. The translation now offered gives the first opportunity English-speaking readers have had to know him in their own language.

ARTHUR MORRISON.

A CHILD OF THE JAGO; a novel of the East End of London, by the author of "Tales of Mean Streets." 12mo. $1.50.

Mr. Morrison is recognized the world over as the most capable man at slum life stories. His "Tales of Mean Streets" was one of the best received books of 1894-95, and the present volume has occupied his time ever since. It is of great force and continuous interest; a book that, once begun, must be finished, and one that will figure as a sensation for a long time to come.

JULIA MAGRUDER.
MISS AYR OF VIRGINIA AND OTHER STORIES. 16mo. $1.25.

Critics have always united in saying of Miss Magruder's work that it was interesting. In addition to this her new volume is noticeable for its grace and beauty, real sentiment where it is needed, and strength as well. It will be welcomed by the many who enjoyed "The Princess Sonia" and "The Violet."

HENRY M. BLOSSOM, Jr.
CHECKERS; a Hard-Luck Story, by the author of "The Documents in Evidence." 16mo. $1.25.
Third edition.

"Abounds in the most racy and picturesque slang."—N. Y. Recorder.

"Checkers is an interesting and entertaining chap, a distinct type, with a separate tongue and a way of saying things that is oddly humorous."—Chicago Record.

"If I had to ride from New York to Chicago on a slow train, I should like half a dozen books as gladsome as Checkers, and I could laugh at the trip."—N. Y. Commercial Advertiser.

ALICE MORSE EARLE.
CURIOUS PUNISHMENTS OF BYGONE DAYS; by the author of "Sabbath in Puritan New England," etc., with many quaint pictures by Frank Hazenplug. 12mo. $1.50.

Mrs. Earle dedicates her book, in the language of an old-time writer, to "All curious and ingenious gentlemen and gentlewomen who can gain from acts of the past a delight in the present days of virtue, wisdom and the humanities."

H. C. CHATFIELD-TAYLOR.

THE LAND OF THE CASTANET; Spanish Sketches, by the author of "Two Women and a Fool," with twenty-five full-page illustrations. 16mo. $1.25.

A collection of rambling sketches of Spanish people and places. Mr. Chatfield-Taylor has written frankly and entertainingly of the most striking features of "The Land of the Castanet." The volume does not pretend to be exhaustive; in no sense is it a guide book—it is intended rather for the person who does not expect to visit Spain than for the traveller.

C. E. RAIMOND.

THE FATAL GIFT OF BEAUTY AND OTHER STORIES, by the author of "George Mandeville's Husband," etc. 16mo. $1.25.

A book of stories which will not quickly be surpassed for real humor, skillful characterization and splendid entertainment. "The Confessions of a Cruel Mistress" is a masterpiece and the "Portman Memmoirs" are exceptionally clever.

GEORGE ADE.

ARTIE; a story of the Streets and Town, with many pictures by John T. McCutcheon. 16mo. $1.25.

These sketches, reprinted from the Chicago Record, attracted great attention on their original appearance. They have been revised and rewritten and in their present form promise to make one of the most popular books of the fall.

LUCAS MALET.

THE CARISSIMA; a novel, by the author of
"The Wages of Sin." 12mo. $1.50.

Few people will have difficulty in remembering the
profound sensation which the publication of "The
Wages of Sin" caused some six years ago. Since that
time Lucas Malet has published no serious work, and
the present volume therefore, represents her best. It
is a novel of intense and continued interest, and will
claim a prominent place among the books of the season.

ALSO

THE CHAP-BOOK.

WHAT IT STANDS FOR.

"The cleverness of this periodical has always amply justified its
existence but the careless reader, who has never taken it seriously, will
be surprised to find on turning over the leaves of this volume how very
much more than merely clever it is. It contains examples of some of
the strongest work that is now being done in letters. It represents the
best tendencies of the younger writers of the day, and, seen in bulk,
even its freaks and excentricities are shown to be representative of their
sort, and are present in it because they are representative, and not
because they are freakish."—St. Paul Globe.

Price, 10 Cents. $2.00 A Year.

Published by HERBERT S. STONE & CO., Chicago.

Herbert S. Stone & Company,
THE CHAP-BOOK.

CHICAGO: The Caxton Building.
LONDON: 10, Norfolk St., Strand.

TELEGRAPHIC ADDRESSES:

"ChapBook, Chicago."
"Editorship, London."

www.ingramcontent.com/pod-product-compliance
Lightning Source LLC
Chambersburg PA
CBHW031018120726
47905CB00007B/1963